CO-ATL-826

WEST GEORGIA REGIONAL LIBRARY SYSTEM
Neva Lomason Memorial Library

A Clinic for Murder

Also by Marsha Landreth

The Holiday Murders

A Dr. Sam Turner Mystery

A Clinic for Murder

Marsha Landreth

Walker and Company
New York

*To Brant and Ross,
tiny babies one day,
strapping men the next*

Copyright © 1993 by Marsha Landreth

All rights reserved. No part of this book may be reproduced or
transmitted in any form or by any means, electronic or mechanical,
including photocopying, recording, or by any information storage and
retrieval system, without permission in writing from the Publisher.

All the characters and events portrayed in this work are fictitious.

First published in the United States of America in 1993
by Walker Publishing Company, Inc.

Published simultaneously in Canada by Thomas Allen & Son
Canada, Limited, Markham, Ontario

Library of Congress Cataloging-in-Publication Data
Landreth, Marsha
A clinic for murder / Marsha Landreth.
(A Dr. Sam Turner mystery)
p.   cm.
ISBN 0-8027-3241-0
1. Women physicians—Wyoming—Fiction. 2. Wyoming—Fiction.
I. Title. II. Series: Landreth, Marsha. Dr. Sam Turner mystery.
PS3562.A4774C58   1993
813'.54—dc20   93-1440
CIP

Printed in the United States of America
2 4 6 8 10 9 7 5 3 1

$\triangledown$

1

"SO HOW'S THE new kid working out?" the eminent Dr. Newman asked as they stepped into the Hotel del Coronado's convention center. Why'd he have to bring up her new partner? They were supposed to be having fun and Eugene was the last thing Sam wanted to think about. Chris was about as cooperative as a dead deer being dragged uphill.

Sam shaded her eyes against the October glare and had a good look at the old goat. Chris had aged noticeably since she'd last seen him seven years back. It worried her, not that she wanted him to know. "Eugene will never replace you or John, but he's not a bad pathologist." She slapped his meaty arm with the convention brochure. "Besides, now I have time to play with you. Speaking of which . . ." She unfolded the program and held it at arm's length. "Toxicology, criminology, odontology, or anthropology?"

He scratched his double chin as if to tell the acolyte he was giving the matter solemn thought. "A walk on the beach?"

The brochure crinkled as her hands flew to her hips. "That was not one of the multiple choices, Christopher Newman. Though I must say, a little exercise might help that monstrous paunch of yours."

Chris sucked in sharply, doing absolutely no good. He looked like the poster child for a Michelin tire in need of a good retread. "It's not as bad as yours, Sam."

Bald-faced lie! She patted six months' worth of pregnancy

that only made her look like she was concealing her bowling ball. "Mine's temporary."

He looked up the stairs to the iron-railed second floor. It kindled her curiosity enough to give a cursory glance. A flock of legs stood in little clusters; soft voices and quiet laughter filtered down. Medical examiners were not, as a whole, outgoing. "I still don't know how you talked me into flying down here, Sam."

"I didn't talk you into coming, you old fart. You talked me into it. Was I yesterday's renowned lecturer? No, not *I.*"

Christopher's benevolent eyes looked heavenward as if in prayerful thanks. "I hate San Diego."

"You are such a grump! Don't know how June puts up with you."

"Puts up with me! She's the one falling apart at the seams. The metal detector at the airport went wild when she walked through. Damn her knee implants."

"Don't be maligning dear sweet June and don't pretend with me. A little sparkle comes into those droopy eyes of yours every time she walks into the room." Sam pinched his rosy cheek. "Think I haven't noticed?"

He rubbed the top of his bald head.

"Don't," she said, pulling his arm away, "it's polished enough."

He smirked. "I could be sitting in my office looking at the Golden Gate Bridge."

"Spare me your troubles. Got enough of my own."

Chris stared hard at her, playfulness replaced with time-honored knowing.

Sam nervously twisted one of the many little blond wisps of new hair that refused to be a part of her ponytail. Not even the largest barrette helped. She wanted him to look away. She hadn't felt this self-conscious since the first day of kindergarten when the teacher made such a fuss over the frilly pink matching dress her twin sister Sharon had forced her to wear. Masking her face from her high cheekbones almost to her jaw was a bright red butterfly tattoo. Not that it was a real tattoo, and her new obstetrician assured her it would go away any day now, but it made her feel like a Christmas tree ornament. And she'd said as much to her obstetrician. Patrick, as sincere as all get-out, told her no one would notice, they'd be blinded by her shiny emerald eyes. What a crock! She preferred Bob's and Ken's teasing to Patrick's sincerity. Not that Bob teased her anymore. If only . . . no sense thinking about all that.

"Why don't you tell John's son?"

"Speaking of something out of left field!"

Chris ran a stubby finger over one of his bushy eyebrows—it was the only hair he could wallow in. "He should be told."

"Don't give me that family-values thing. If you remember, it cost somebody the presidency." Two doctors came in out of the blinding sun. Sam waited for the door to close. She didn't feel like yelling over the early morning traffic noises. *Feel* was the operative word. The vile sweetness of the perennially blooming flowers along the pathway was doing her in and she had to concentrate hard on not throwing up.

Sam opened the collar of the white blouse peeking out from under her denim jumper to get more air. Pressing a finger to Chris's well-padded bright red Hawaiian shirt—Chris was right about one thing, they were dressed more for a walk on the beach than a medical examiners' convention—she said, "Listen, you old goat, you live your life and I'll live mine."

"I have half a notion to tell him myself."

Her good-natured kidding ended and her eyes slanted in his direction. "You do, and our friendship is over." She scanned the brochure, unwilling and unable to look him in the face. "Besides, Jeffrey might be the father."

"Okay, Sam, now that you've brought it up. What's the real story?"

"Nothing to tell. Jeffrey said something that only the murderer could have known. How else was I going to get blood, skin tissue, and seminal samples without making him suspicious?"

"But he wasn't the killer."

"And the samples proved it." She didn't like the I-told-you-so look on his face. "But he was an accomplice." This was still a sore subject with her and nothing she wanted to talk about. Jeffrey, her one-time best friend and confidante, was locked up tight. He had to have known better. He was, after all, the county attorney. Telling the killer she knew who did it was her undoing. But why did she have to justify all this to Chris? "And that's all I'm ever going to say about it."

"Criminology," Chris said as he took her arm and led her up the stairs. "I'm sure that's the one you're most interested in." The sarcasm in his voice could have wilted the plastic palm tree on the landing. "If I'd known that's what you were up to, I'd never have returned your call, Dr. Turner. You gave new meaning to DNA fingerprinting."

Same kept her eyes on the pattern in the red carpet as they climbed.

"You should have gone to the police, that's what they're there for."

Not to her way of thinking. The incompetent nincompoops. Not that she didn't make a mess of things herself. "I was going to . . . as soon as I had the DNA matchup. I needed some evidence, for chrissakes. The end."

Chris raised a shaggy brow. "You could have gotten AIDS, Sam. It was dumb." The doctor in line ahead of her glanced over his shoulder.

"I tested the specimens from the murder victim," she said for everyone's information. The eavesdropping doctor scribbled his name and lit out. Sam signed her name more legibly. She needed the continuing education credit certificate.

"Even if you had had the right suspect—which you didn't—you still took a chance."

She glanced around for the meeting room. "This way," she said, pointing, after he had signed in. She was all for a change of subject.

"He could have been newly infected."

"I don't live in San Francisco. There were only forty HIV positives in all of Wyoming at the time."

"Forty! Hard to believe. I see that many new cases each day."

"Do we have to talk shop? We're supposed to be having fun." The curtains in the conference room were drawn. They waited at the door for their eyes to adjust.

"We could be outside in the sunshine and fresh air instead of this dark, smoky room. Let's consider the health of the little side effect of your detective work."

Sam gave him a stern look, which she suspected he couldn't see; he was nothing more than a shadow himself. He was right, of course—she had no business trying to play detective and she would never do it again. If it hadn't have been for Derek she would have been killed. But she wasn't about to admit it to Chris and she wasn't about to take any more grief about what's good for the baby. "I'm thirty-four years old, Christopher Newman. If I want to be a single parent, that's *my* business."

Chris put sausage fingers to the small of her back. "There are two seats in the back row. We can sneak out and take that walk on the beach—for my health—if it's boring."

"And not stay for the midmorning break? I thought you liked their pastries. You ate enough of them yesterday morning." She smiled over her shoulder.

"Being pregnant's made you mean."

Sam loved Chris like a father. Hard to believe he was the same age as her late husband. How she missed working with the two of them! She thought she would never get over the loss of John. But for the last year the face in her dreams hadn't been John's, but his son's. She couldn't be held responsible for her dreams, but Derek had crept into her thoughts—something she should have been able to control. Seven years of widowhood was a long time. Seven years. She'd almost forgotten the smell of salt air, the bent and twisted trees along the shoreline, fog, the BART, operas, Golden Gate Park, Candlestick Park, a hospital big enough to get lost in, and John's face. She plopped down on the rigid chair and rummaged through her purse looking for a Kleenex. "Also blind." Sam wiped a vagrant tear from her cheek with the back of her hand and threw her purse on what was left of Chris's lap after his stomach spilled over. "See if you can find my glasses."

"How am I supposed to see anything in this dark room?" Chris pawed through the wreckage. "Why don't you wear them on a chain around your neck?"

"Like a little old lady? No thanks." She put her nose in the purse. "See them?"

"You've got your head in the way, Sam." He yanked the purse away. "They're not here. Want me to go to your room after them?"

"Why? You wouldn't come back!"

"Yes, I would. I can sleep just as well here."

The room grew quiet as a stately white-haired lecturer headed toward the podium. "Just don't snore," Sam whispered.

He did snore. Dr. Sommers, the noted forensic pathologist from Johns Hopkins, had barely started the slide show before Sam was elbowing Chris.

". . . there is mystery in every death until the cause is known. Each investigator must ask whether the death was natural or unnatural, homicide, suicide, or accident?"

"Chris," Sam hissed. "For chrissakes, stop snoring."

"What? What?"

"Shh," she whispered. "You were snoring."

"Sorry," he whispered back, folding his arms over his barrel chest and resting his heavy head on Sam's shoulder.

"A coroner is a medical detective, specifically trained to solve the mystery." The speaker clicked up a slide of a slight man half-suspended by a rope wound around his throat and body in a figure eight and thrown over the shower rod, the other end tied around his wrist. "Suicide? Murder? Accident?"

There was some debate, but it was the little thumping on the inside wall of her uterus that held Sam's attention. She smiled, thinking about Patrick returning to the examining room after giving her time to dress. Nothing was more humiliating than having to listen to a lecture with one hand clutching a blue paper slip-on gown with northern exposure. Of course, she had already run the test and knew she was pregnant, and he knew she knew she was pregnant, but she knew he would still make the announcement and probably lecture her. So when instead of the lecture, Patrick asked her to marry him, Sam all but fell off the examining table she had so casually draped a leg over. Patrick was nice enough, but he could never be anything more than a friend.

A sharp kick to the ribs returned her to the present. Sam rubbed her hand over the tiny being and pushed the palm of her hand against the offending foot. *I'm happy you came along, but could you please not kick me in the ribs again.*

The discussion ended and the speaker said, "Accident. A case of autoerotic asphyxia. The victim hoped to obtain orgasm by risking death. Unfortunately, he slipped into unconsciousness and then into death."

"And missed the big O," Chris whispered. So the old goat was awake.

"In my practice, I see thirty to forty deaths a year attributed to autoerotic asphyxia," the speaker went on.

The next was a picture of a young man sprawled out on a bed, a vial and needle on the night stand. "Suicide, murder, or accident?"

The discussion concluded with the theory of accidental death caused by an overdose.

"Murder," the forensic pathologist said. "The needle went straight up the vein. If the syringe had been held by the victim, the needle would have been injected at a right angle. Hence, murder."

She could have taken issue with that statement; it only proved the injection was administered by another person.

Sam saw a stir of motion along the side as a couple of people started to leave. Light from the open door flooded across the screen. "How rude!" she whispered to Chris.

"Bet they're going for a walk on the beach."

The next slide was of a young woman sprawled over a rock on a beach below a sharp cliff. "Accident, suicide, or murder?"

Sam jumped to her feet. "Murder."

The lecturer looked in the direction of the voice. "Murder, someone said. Why?"

Sam raised her voice over the projector's whine. "Rigidity is maintaining the legs in an unnatural position. The force of gravity should have molded her body around the rock if she had fallen to her death. She was thrown over the cliff several hours after she expired."

"Correct. And, in the case of possible homicide, this example emphasizes the necessity of making observations before a body is moved." He clicked to the next slide, a picture of a death-blackened man and a nondiscolored woman.

Chris leaned over and whispered, "There'll be no living with you, now."

Sam cupped a hand over her mouth as she whispered back, "Had a case just like that last winter. Young kid. Legs were flexed like he'd been sitting in a chair and the rigor was broken in his finger where his uncle placed the gun in his hand. Real sad. The guy killed his wife and three little kids as well."

"What happened to him?"

Before she had a chance to speak, a blurred figure on the aisle a few rows up fell to the floor, and people started moving quickly. "Turn on the light!" someone yelled frantically.

The response was immediate.

Sam stood to see. "Excuse me," she said sliding past Chris. "Excuse me," she told the wiry man on Chris's other side. And so on until she ran freely down the side aisle. Sam fell to her knees beside the fiftyish man. As a small-town pathologist, she logged a great many hours in the E.R. Probably more than anyone else in the room, filled with specialists.

"Give him some room," she bellowed as she yanked the tie from around his neck and ripped open his white shirt.

She caught someone's eye. "You call an ambulance." She felt her patient's weak, thready pulse. "Just hang on." She looked at the circle of concerned faces. Each would know what to do as soon as he stopped breathing. At least they could solve the mystery of why he stopped breathing. This was better than a slide show. She turned her attention back to the patient. "The paramedics will be here in a jiffy." She tried to sound reassuring. *Just don't arrest on me!*

The man mumbled something. Sam lowered her ear to his mouth. "Murder . . . letter in safe . . . authorities . . ."

"What?"

His hand fell away as he arrested.

"Did he say something?" asked a freckle-faced redhead. He couldn't have been much more than a medical student.

"Ah . . ." Sam shook her head. "Nothing I understood." She turned back to the matter at hand. "Can someone help me with compressions?"

Another young doctor fell to his knees at her side. "Just finished a rotating internship," he said as he felt for the sternum. "This is the first thing I've felt comfortable with since I arrived."

Sam jerked the arresting doctor's head back and blew two long breaths into his mouth.

"I've been working on the railroad . . ." the intern sang. Using the rhythm of the tune in place of counting compressions was a novel approach.

Sam blew into his mouth.

"All the long lost day . . ."

Sam took a deep breath and exhaled into the ashen-faced man's mouth.

"I've been working on the railroad . . ."

Sam emptied her lungs around the man's mouth.

"Just to pass the time away . . ."

Sam pinched off the nose again, and pushed air into his mouth.

Murder, he said.

2

SAM WAITED UNTIL the gurney was placed into the silent ambulance before she jerked Chris around the corner and headed for the hotel's main entrance.

She slipped Chris's Welcome to San Diego name tag out of the plastic holder pinned to his shirt.

"What are you doing?" Chris asked, as he grabbed for his property.

Sam slapped his hand. "Just be still." She looked at the doorman as she stuck the name tag into her pocket. She took another one out and slipped it into the holder.

"You all right, Sam?" Chris looked down at the tag. "Wait a minute. This isn't mine."

"Chris, shut up." She took his arm and propelled him toward the lobby. "Just go along with whatever I say."

"What are you doing? What're you going to say?"

"I have no idea. Now shush!"

"And who's Doyle Smith?"

"The dead man," she whispered as they passed the doorman. "And unless you want to be one too, hush."

"Okaaaaaaaay," he said, his voice trilling an octave.

They walked toward the registration desk at the left of the door and watched three clerks move in circles. The heavy activity was around the corner of the L-shaped counter where departing guests were lined up to kingdom come.

Sam and Chris stood under the check-in sign. It made more sense.

"Be right with you." A dark-haired man continued to sift through a file of receipts.

"No hurry," Sam lied, smiling broadly. She turned around and casually leaned both arms against the counter, pretending interest in the shopping area of the majestic lobby. "How much do you think that evening gown costs, Doyle?"

Chris didn't reply.

She punched him in the ribs to get his attention.

Chris jumped. "Oh, ah . . ." He looked at the dress in the boutique window. "A hundred dollars?"

"More likely five."

"Five dollars?"

"Hundred."

"Hundred! Who'd pay five hundred dollars for one outfit?"

"Not me."

Chris swallowed hard. "Don't let June see it."

A harassed-looking clerk approached. "Ma'am?"

"Doyle, here, has left the key in his room."

"No problem." He summoned an elderly bellboy. "He'll show you to your room."

"That would be wonderful." It would have been wonderful except for one little detail. Sam turned to Chris. "Why don't you go sit on one of those comfy red-velvet circular jobbies for a second, Doyle?"

"And miss this?" he grumbled as he headed across the lobby.

When he was out of earshot, she turned and smiled. First at the bellboy, and then the clerk. "You see, Doyle, my father-in-law, has Alzheimer's disease. He doesn't always remember things. Not only has he forgotten his key, he's forgotten his room number as well."

The men stared at her, then at each other. In her condition even the most suspicious wouldn't profile her as a cat burglar. She hoped.

"And you don't remember, either?" the clerk asked.

Sam's smile slipped away as the heat of a blush burnt her

red butterfly. "I—I just arrived." Sam pointed to Chris, who was trying to look at his name tag upside down. She sighed. "Poor Dad doesn't even remember his name."

"He's been here all alone?" the clerk asked in a tone of disapproval.

They weren't cutting her much slack. "No, Mom's here with him. She's probably up in the room . . . wherever that may be." She could almost see the light bulb over her head. "Maybe you could call their room, make sure—see if Mom answers?"

He did, but there was no answer. Fortunately.

"Mom's probably on the beach. She just loves the ocean."

The men alternated between having their heads together and staring at Chris, who was still very interested in his name tag. The desk clerk was satisfied. "Six six two nine."

"Dad," Sam called. When he didn't look up, she smiled sweetly at the bellboy. "Guess he forgot I'm his daughter."

"In-law."

Her whole face must have been red if heat was any indication. "Daughter-in-law. Be right back." She ran over and grabbed Chris. "Come one, we're going up."

Sam started Chris toward the elevator. "In the tower building," the clerk called. Chris and she whirled around and followed the bellboy out the door.

The doorman of the hotel's high-rise addition greeted the bellboy as they entered. "Charlie."

"Frank."

"No luggage?"

Charlie hunched his shoulders. "Mister Smith, here, got locked out. Mrs. Turner, here—" He stopped abruptly and pointed to her name tag. "You don't have the same name."

"Dr. Turner, Mrs. Smith." Why hadn't she thought to say Doyle was her father? She could have simply said Turner was her married name. She didn't have Derek's knack for lying. "Professional name. It's a women's lib thing."

Chris rolled his eyes in appreciation.

Frank gave a who-am-I-to-care kind of sigh.

The elevator took longer than Wyoming's winter months. Sam, with Chris in tow and Charlie sauntering behind them, snaked through the sixth-floor corridors, stopping once for Charlie to tell the Latino maid to keep her cart closer to the wall. Centuries later, they were at Doyle's door.

Sam nimbly blocked Charlie's way as he started to step in. She shoved a five into his withered palm. "Thanks ever so much." She whisked Chris through the aperture and slammed the door. "Shit!" she added as she leaned against the closed door.

"What are we doing here, Sam? This is illegal." A singsong cadence crept into his voice. "I think we could go to jail. I know we could go to jail. We're going to go to jail. Sam, let's get out of here."

"Just let me catch my breath." Sam took a couple of steps through the foyer until she had a sweeping view of the modern room. "Shit!"

"What is it?" Chris looked over her shoulder. "Messy man," he added after seeing the disheveled room. "Even the pictures are crooked."

Sam turned around and glared at him. "Sherlock you're not. His room's been trashed. Make that their room."

"A wife? I didn't see anyone go with the body."

"She probably doesn't know yet."

"Let's get out of here before she comes back."

"She's probably on the spouses' La Jolla shopping tour with June. Won't be back for hours." Sam stepped around the dumped suitcase, the scattered clothing, and the twisted bedspread half-hiding the wadded sheets, and made her way to the muted blue plaid drapes. The light rushed in as she pulled back the curtain. "Look at the view. Wall-to-wall ocean." Her own turn-of-the-century room had a commanding view of the parking lot. She opened the sliding glass door to the smell of salty sea air. Sam looked out over the blue—so blue it hurt her eyes—ocean to where it merged with the sky. She took a long deep breath and stepped to the balcony rail. The sun worshipers on the white sandy beach six stories down looked like tiny dolls. So did the Navy SEALs practicing maneuvers off shore.

Chris was beside her. "Let's go."

"Look at them, Chris."

"You're incorrigible."

"Look!" she demanded.

He shaded his eyes against the glare. "Ah, to look like that again."

Sam smiled, "Chris, my dear, you never looked like that."

"When you were in diapers. Now let's go."

Sam looked him up and down. "I'll give you the benefit of the doubt."

"Gee, thanks," he muttered.

She leaned over and kissed his wrinkled forehead. "It's what's inside that counts. And I'm sure there are two very nice people in there."

He cleared his throat. "Ditto. Now let's get out of here."

Their short interlude ended as she remembered Doyle Smith's dying words. "We're looking for a letter. It's in the safe. Though it looks like we're a tad late." She walked through the wreckage to the closet next to the door. "My room's safe is . . . aha! . . . right here." She dumped the contents of her purse on the blue carpet and sifted through until she found her key. "Think you can move out of my light?"

Chris mumbled as he stepped aside. "Sam, let's get out of here! What if his wife simply went for a walk on the beach?"

"Doesn't fit, damn."

"So, let's get out of here."

She scooped up her belongings and threw them back into her bag. "Look in the bathroom while I go through his clothes. We need to find the key."

His eyes rolled back on tilt as he mopped beads of sweat from his forehead. "Sam, we've got to get out of here."

"If you don't help, it'll just take that much longer."

Resignedly, Chris got down on his hands and knees to retrieve the spilled shaving and make up kits in the bathroom. "This is breaking and entering, for petesakes."

She walked to the bathroom door. "Want to yell it a little louder? Doubt if those handsome Navy divers heard. Besides, it's already been broken into. We're just checking to see what's missing. He asked me to deliver the letter to the authorities. I'm just looking for it."

Chris groaned.

A wet towel tangled around Chris's leg and started to slide, threatening to tumble a small decanter that teetered on the edge of the vanity. "Don't move!"

"What? What?" Chris jumped up, sending the bottle over the side. Sam dove for it, spilling the liquid on her jumper.

"Goddammit, Chris. Didn't I tell you not to move?" She stuck the stopper back into the neck of the bottle.

Chris sniffed the air. "That stinks."

"A little dab will do you, that's for sure." Sam twirled the perfume around. "Read French?"

"I'm a doctor, I took Latin. What does it say?"

Sam held it at arm's length. "I don't know, I'm a doctor, too. All I know is that it was concocted in Paris, France." She placed it on the vanity. "Maybe she won't notice that a bit spilled."

Chris sniffed. "Only if she's lost her sense of smell."

Sam wiped her hand over the wet spot on her jumper. "And this is my favorite outfit."

"Favorite! You own another dress?"

"Yeah, I do. That is, the radiologist's wife loaned me her maternity clothes. Unlike some people I know, I won't be wearing fat clothes forever."

He tugged his Hawaiian shirt down. "I'm ready to go whenever you are."

"Well, I'm not. So far all we know about Doyle is that his wife has expensive taste. Get busy."

Sam copied Doyle's address from the suitcase tag. "He's from Denver. What do you know?"

"Was. He's dead now."

Sam pulled a scrap of paper from the wastebasket and carried it to the bathroom. "Found a clue maybe. A phone number . . . no area code, though." She shoved it into her pocket.

"Can we leave now?"

"No!"

There was a knock at the door. "Housekeeping."

"Great!" Chris said too loudly.

"Shh." As one would go to her own execution, Sam walked toward the door. The metal of the master key clanged against the brass lock. "Just a moment, please." Sam noticed Chris plastered against the bathroom wall like three-dimensional red-flowered wallpaper. She motioned for him to close the bathroom door. He didn't. "Yes?" Sam hollered through the door.

The voice mumbled something about cleaning the room.

Sam's heart pounded faster than she could think. "Could you clean another room and come back? Dad's still stinking up the bathroom." Out of the corner of her eye she saw Chris mouth his thanks. She shrugged.

"Si."

Sam listened to the squeaky wheels of the cart as it rolled sluggishly by. The knock was at the neighbor's door. Sam tiptoed toward the bathroom. "Let's straighten up and get out of here."

"Didn't I already say that?"

$\triangledown$

3

Sam took a deep breath before stepping into the massive dome-shaped dining room, smelling only Mrs. Smith's nauseating perfume. Her denim jumper would probably stink to high heaven all the way up to the baby's arrival.

The tuxedoed whatever-he-was-called looked up from his reservation book. "Yes, ma'am?"

She searched the room. "I see my party, thanks anyway."

"Allow me to—"

Sam skirted him, moved between the tables, ducked under a server's tray, and stood beside the huge round table occupied by all the illustrious guest speakers. She nodded to Chris, who gulped his food and shoveled in a new forkful, no doubt thinking she was about to drag him away.

"Dr. Sommers?"

The distinguished doctor from Johns Hopkins looked up, his gray eyes inquiring.

"I'm sorry to bother you, sir," Sam noticed Chris sliding down in his chair, "but it's most urgent that I speak with you . . . immediately."

Dr. Sommers took the napkin from his lap and dropped it into the chair as he rose. "Of course, Dr. Turner," he said after a quick glance at her name tag. He followed silently behind her until they were in the lobby. "You're the doctor who administered the CPR to poor Smith. Very impressive."

"Not as impressive as if I'd saved him." The lobby was filled with people. "Would you mind if we talked as we walked?"

They wandered along the concrete walk that led to one of the swimming pools. "The coroner's releasing Smith's body without an autopsy."

"So?" He kicked a pebble out of his path.

Sam took a deep breath of the wet sea air and coughed.

"Are you all right?" he asked as he gave her a good thump on the back.

She nodded, but it still took a moment before she could speak. "I believe he was murdered."

It was he who coughed this time. More out of embarrassment, Sam feared. He probably thought she was nuts. He held up his hand, telling her to give him a minute. "Sorry." He cleared his throat. "Reason?" he finally asked in the true manner of a seasoned investigator.

"He told me so. With his dying breath, he whispered, 'murder.' " No reason to tell him the rest, just in case her trust was misplaced.

"In that case," he seized her arm, "we'd better listen to him." He hustled her back to the entrance and into a taxi, which had just dropped off two young ladies carrying identical Louis Vuitton purses.

The elevator opened deep within the bowels of the hospital. Sam and Dr. Sommers followed the multicolored lines running along the walls. It was the yellow line they were told to track to the autopsy suites. They lost the blue line at the first corner, the red at the next intersection.

"Boy, wouldn't Larry die to see this place?"

"Sorry?" Dr. Sommers asked.

"What?"

"Did you say something?"

"If I did, I was talking out loud to myself. Senility, I guess."

The stately gentleman squeezed her elbow. "I don't believe that for a minute."

Sam didn't mention that her father was rotting away in a nursing home with Alzheimer's and unless someone came up with a cure in the next twenty years or so, she had a

better-than-average chance of ending up the same way. It
was a fine legacy to be giving the baby.

"Larry's your husband?"

"Heavens no!"

Sommers chuckled. "Ex, I take it?"

"Hospital administrator."

"Worse."

They exchanged smiles.

"We've passed eternity and I still don't see the light at the
end of yellow," she said, weary to her marrow.

"Big place." He nodded to her bowling ball. "Do you need
to rest?"

"No, I'm just impressed. I have to go to the funeral home
to do an autopsy."

"Where do you practice?"

"Sheridan, Wyoming. Population fifteen thousand. And
claiming to be the third largest town in the state. State's
population is four-hundred thousand," she added in true
Chamber-of-Commerce tradition.

Sommers opened one of the bay doors leading into the
autopsy suites.

Sam stopped just inside and gave an appreciative whistle.
It contained a stainless-steel table, a weighing scale, sink
with faucet, electrical saw, a television monitor, a microphone, and other state-of-the-art equipment. She looked
through the window to another suite boasting four stainless-steel tables and like equipment. She'd forgotten big-city
medicine. Even the smell was different. Although many of
the bodies were embalmed here—hard telling when or if
someone will come looking for a John Doe—the walls didn't
reek of formaldehyde like they did in the preparation room
at the funeral home in Sheridan.

Doyle's body was stretched out on the steel table. He had
a noticeable broken rib. She thought she had heard a crack
between *been* and *working*.

Dr. Sommers placed a firm hand on her shoulder. "You
did a fine job. I couldn't have done it."

Sam looked up at him. "You could if you practiced in Sheridan."

They found the forensic pathologist sitting in a sound-proof booth drinking from a coffee mug. He looked up when Sommers's long shadow was cast over him. He opened the glass door. "Ah, Dr. Sommers, Dr. Turner, I'm Dr. Jenkins, deputy medical examiner."

Sommers shook the outstretched hand. "David Sommers, Johns Hopkins."

"I worked with a Johns Hopkins resident, Marty Green."

"Oh, yes, I remember him. Good man." Sommers, Sam's paradigm of a perfect gentleman, turned his attention to Sam as if to tell the host doctor it was time for him to do the same.

Sam smiled and gave him a determined hand but mumbled, "Sam Turner, Sheridan County Coroner." Johns Hopkins is a hard act to follow.

"Coffee?" Jenkins asked.

Both of them declined.

"The photos." He craned around and picked up the pile with his free hand.

"Thanks." Sam took them, trying to square them at the same time. The first picture was of Doyle fully clothed, except for the tie Sam had removed. They continued as his clothing, layer after layer, was removed. "Could we look at his personal effects first?"

Jenkins shrugged. "If you wish." As if to say, "What good would that do?"

The threesome walked through the long hall to an intersecting corridor and finally into the screened-off property room. After Jenkins signed the log, the attendant produced a rectangular plastic box containing the decedent's belongings. Jenkins gave Sam a look as if to say that she was wasting his valuable time.

When Sam had everything out on the table, she reached for her purse. "Can't see a thing without my glasses," she announced, rummaging through her purse. "I'm going to start wearing my glasses on a chain around my neck like a little old lady."

As she put on her glasses, she spilled the decedent's watch, wallet, and coins onto the floor. "Oops," she said as she watched both men gather up the scattered effects.

"There. No harm's been done." Sommers said as he laid the change next to a key to a safe.

"Nothing here that I see." Sam looked up, "Dr. Sommers?"

"I'm satisfied."

In the autopsy suite Sam and Sommers sat on stools and observed as Jenkins covered every square inch of the decedent's body with a magnifying glass. "I don't see a needle puncture."

Sam sighed. "There has to be one."

Worry lines deepened Sommers's brow. "Perhaps he was confused and was remembering one of the cases I was presenting?"

"No," Sam said without explanation.

Sommers got up and leaned over the body. "Do you mind if I try something?"

Jenkins pulled back and held up his hands in a contemptuous be-my-guest gesture. If Sommers noticed, he pretended otherwise; he put his hands around the corpse's left arm just below the shoulder and squeezed. Nothing. He repeated the procedure on the right side. A tiny drop of blood appeared on the back of Doyle Smith's hand. "What do you know?"

The other doctor placed the magnifying glass over the hand. "Good needle."

Sommers returned to his stool. "Feel vindicated?"

"So far."

▽

4

"Sam, I was trying to take in some sun," Chris said as he clip-clopped along behind her on his plastic thongs.

"Sun's bad for you." Sam pushed through the glass door into the tower lobby. "You know that."

Chris tugged at the seat of his plaid swimming trunks. "I'll be dead before skin cancer has time to settle in. Kind of like taking away cigarettes from a dying man."

Sam laughed a little too loudly and looked over at the doorman who was watching them. "Where's Frank?"

"Gone home." He turned to watch a woman and two little children track sand in from the beach. When they disappeared down the hall, he said, "You'd think they didn't know what those shower heads are for."

Sam nodded agreeably. "Some people."

"I see all kinds . . . you wouldn't believe."

"Actually, I would. By the way, Dad left the key in the room. Could I bother you to let us in?"

"No problem," he said as he hoisted himself off his chair and rounded the counter.

This time the elevator doors opened as soon as Sam pressed the button. Sam listened patiently as Frank's replacement went on and on about the weirdos.

"Come on . . . Dad."

Chris looked wistfully at the retaining wall as if he could see the Pacific Ocean beyond it, pursed his lips, and clomped into the elevator. Frank Number Two went on and on as they rode up. He was still talking when they got off.

"Just last week—"

"No, this way," Sam pulled on his uniformed arm.

"Oh. One of the ocean-view rooms."

"Lovely view. Isn't it . . . Dad?"

"Peachy keen," Chris answered, showing about as much enthusiasm as a little boy playing dolls with his sisters.

Sam shoved a five into the attendant's palm and slid behind the door. "Thanks so much."

"Thank you!"

"Dad—" She jerked Chris inside, closed the door, stuck her hand into her pocket, and pulled out a tiny key. "Here's the key I stole from the effects box at the morgue. We can break into the safe now." She slid the closet door open and pushed back the clothes.

"Sam?"

"Just a minute. I've almost got it . . . there."

"Sam?" Christopher was getting to be a regular scale triller.

"Airline tickets and a wad of money. It's not here!"

"And what were you looking for, ma'am?"

Sam whirled around to see a policeman standing beside Chris. For the first time, she could hear the grieving widow's sobs coming from the balcony.

"Yes, I understand my rights. And no, I do not need an attorney." Sam tapped her fingers along the side of the interrogation table. Cops were so stupid. "Do I look like a criminal?"

The detective blew the hair off his forehead in disgust. "Ted Bundy didn't look like much of a criminal."

Sam's eyes were slits. "Look. The man keels over. He tells me he's been murdered and to get the letter out of the safe and see that it gets to the authorities. That's all I was doing."

He laced his hands behind his head, showing gargantuan rings of perspiration under his arms. "Breaking and entering? You admitted stealing the key to the safe from the forensic center. And where's this letter?"

She shrugged. "The people who ransacked the room earlier must have taken it."

"The officer at the scene didn't notice it had been ransacked. Nor had the widow."

"That's because I cleaned up when I was there the first time."

The man looked up at the mirror that Sam guessed was a viewing window. "Guess you should explain it all to the judge."

"Fine. Let's go see him."

He stood and walked to the door. "In the morning."

"Fine," Sam said as she too stood. "I'll see him in the morning. Now if that's all, I'd like to go back to the hotel."

"I'm afraid you'll have to be our guest for the night."

$\triangledown$

5

"TURNER SAMANTHA TURNER."

Sam got off the filthy bunk and rushed to the bars. "Over here." She divided her attention between the approaching woman guard and her roommates, who looked like they had come from a Halloween party. She had a sneaking suspicion as to their occupation and why they were spending the night as guests of the city.

The jailer or deputy or whatever her official title might have been unlocked the door. "You're free to go. Pick up your personal effects at the desk."

Sam pointed the way she'd been brought in. "That way?"

The woman nodded. "Only one way out, dearie."

Sam nodded her thanks and headed for the door. She made a beeline for the desk and cleared her throat. "I'd like my things . . . Samantha Turner."

The uniformed man looked across the counter contemptuously before hacking up a wad of greenish sputum and spitting into an unseen wastebasket. She *hoped* there was a wastebasket by his feet.

"I trust you're on antibiotics."

He picked up a huge envelope. Surely she hadn't done anything to deserve the disdainful look on his face. He spread the contents of the envelope over the countertop and had her check off everything. "Everything there?"

"Seems to be."

He turned the clipboard around. "Then put your John Henry at the bottom."

As she signed, she asked, "And what of Dr. Newman? Is he being released also?"

"His mouthpiece got him out hours ago."

So how come she was still here? She pushed the clipboard back to him. "Thanks." She dumped her junk into her purse and hurried out before they changed their minds.

She had pushed through the doors before she saw the shadowy figure leaning against the railing down the middle of the stairs; recognition came almost simultaneously. Even at rest Derek Turner exhibited a military bearing and a catlike awareness. The quickening in her stomach lasted a great deal longer than she cared to admit. She couldn't think what to do. Going back to jail held a certain appeal. But he'd come for her, and most likely he was the reason she'd been released.

Sam squared her shoulders and held her chin high—maybe a little too high—as she started down the stairs. She fiddled with the strap of her purse as she passed him.

He flipped his cigarette to the concrete step and reached out for her arm. "Come on, I'll take you home."

"I'm not going home," Sam said a little less calmly than she had intended.

Burning fingers tightened around her arm. "To the hotel."

She pulled away as she continued down the steps. "Chris called you?"

"Aunt June." She wasn't really his aunt. John Turner and Chris had been partners since getting out of residency, and their families had been close. It pounded home the notion that she was the outsider.

"Well, strike her name from my Christmas card list."

There was a taxi waiting, of course. Sam slid across the plastic seat until her shoulder nudged the far door. She resisted the angry impulse to snap the door open and run. What would it get her? He'd just follow.

She couldn't keep her eyes from straying to his reflected profile on the window. No insight could be garnered from his expressionless face. It was always his way, never let the other guy get the advantage. He ran a hand through his disheveled, thick, dark hair. He looked tired. Who didn't? Her head throbbed tightly. She reminded herself that he'd lied to her, that he wasn't the man he pretended to be.

So what if her brain kept producing phenylethylamine, dopamine, and norepinephrine whenever he was around? The endorphins were nice, too, but she could get that sense of security by taking morphine if she wanted, which she didn't. And why should she be surprised that her pituitary gland secreted oxytocin? Hadn't John evoked feelings of euphoria, security, and peace, and cuddling attachment? Why wouldn't her genetic imprinting trigger the same romantic reactions toward the son who was the spitting image of the man she had loved with all her heart?

Just say no.

When the taxi stopped in front of the hotel, Sam bolted for the door. "Thanks for the ride, Derek. Goodnight."

Derek paid the driver and followed her in. "Want a drink?"

"Gee, Derek, doubt if the bar's open at—" she ostentatiously looked at her watch—"four o'clock in the morning. But thanks just the same."

She pushed the elevator UP button with repeated frenzy. The doors creaked open and she jumped aboard. "Goodnight." Derek stepped in. Sam kept her eyes glued to the floor indicator, ready to bolt when they reached the third floor. "Goodnight," she whispered as they both got off. Derek took a key from his pocket and unlocked her door. "Where'd you get a key to *my* room?"

"At the front desk."

"Showed them your superspy badge or something?" Sam stepped into the dark room.

"My driver's license. You still have one?" Derek ran a hand along the wall, feeling for the light switch.

"Of course," she answered, throwing her purse on the dresser. Wyoming wouldn't take a doctor's driver's license away, even with her dubious record—albeit unjustified. "What did you tell them?"

"That I was Derek Turner and I wanted another key to Samantha Turner's room."

She kicked his empty soft-sided suitcase out of her way as she inspected the corner of her room. He was so infuriating. She wanted to be angry with him if only to vent her own frustrations. No, she was angry. She had good reason to be angry. He'd lied! "You look tan. Been covering a *story* in the Antarctic?"

"Middle East." He disappeared into the bathroom and returned with a Kleenex. "I've never known you to have a tissue when you needed one." So something was irritating her eyes. Big deal. Did he have to glide his hand across her back? "Shall we talk about it, or go to bed?"

Sam fingered the broadcloth curtains. Did he have to be so damned solicitous?

"Fine." He moved to the bed and turned down the covers. "I'm going to bed."

That was her bed! Angrily Sam turned around. "No, let's talk. I can understand why you first came to Sheridan and why you pretended to be a journalist . . . but why did you have to lie? Why did you have to pretend to be in . . ." She turned back to the curtains, her resolve gone.

"To be in love with you?" He leaned into her, supporting his hands on the wall behind her. "I wasn't pretending. I loved you as much then as I do now."

She ducked under his arms, yanked her 49ers nightshirt out of the drawer, and headed for the bathroom. Hansel dutifully picked up the trail of static-charged underwear. She gripped the knob on the bathroom door hard enough to leave an imprint along her palm. "Slipping away after my funeral without even so much as a good-bye wasn't a great way of proving it."

"The whole thing had gotten so out of hand. And it was a local matter. Getting out of town was about the only alternative left. Besides, you told me you never wanted to see me again as long as you lived."

"And I still don't!" Sam slammed the bathroom door.

Sam sat on the toilet seat watching the water pour into

the tub and a tremor shake her hands. The whole dirty business rushed back to her. Why had they called him? In a few hours' time the judge would have freed her. She didn't need Derek. For anything. She slipped down into the warm bathwater until she was totally submerged, but even soothing water couldn't settle her anxiety.

"Samantha?"

She grabbed for the yellow towel as Derek came through the door. "Think I can have a little privacy?"

Derek all but tore his windbreaker pocket trying to free a pack of Camels. Half-a-dozen cigarettes fell to the floor as he tapped the bottom of the pack. The match flared on the fourth try. The cross-country flight had taken its toll. He touched the fluttering flame to the tip of his cigarette and inhaled deeply. Sam watched him pull on his pacifier again. Didn't he care what he was doing to his lungs?

He lifted the lid of the toilet and flicked ashes into the artificially blue water. He leaned against the sink and stared down at her. She could feel his eyes burning through the towel that had molded itself to her body. What was she going to say to him?

"That towel's not going to do you much good wet and I doubt if we'll be able to get another one before morning."

She fingered the little printed crown above the words *Hotel del Coronado*. "You'd think a classy place like this would embroider their crest instead of stamping it on."

Derek pulled on the cigarette and blew out three impressive smoke rings. "So how's the puppy?"

"The Little One's fine and so's Fido." She unscrewed the sample-sized bottle of shampoo. Did he think her fat?

"Fido?"

"Jeffrey's puppy." She squeezed the liquid gel over her head. The room was filled with smoke now, polluting the air she would pass on to the baby. "They're about eighty-five pounds."

He nodded. "Practically grown. Jeffrey really named the poor thing Fido?"

Sam smiled despite herself.

"How's Jake doing?" He seemed intent on continuing with polite small talk. She'd prefer him sleeping in her bed to this.

"Better. Emil, his nephew, is helping out."

Derek nodded. "That deer of yours?"

Would he never stop? "Haven't seen Alfred. Hope he comes around before hunting season opens."

"Any new bison?"

She rubbed her lather with a fury. "Had two in the spring just after you left and picked up two adults in Dallas a couple months back. Found the ranch through your feature story." She assumed a superspy could detect the accusation in her voice.

"You know, it wasn't my idea to go to Sheridan. The Witness Protection Agency asked for my help." He looked up at the ceiling as he took a long breath. Sam suspected he was counting to ten. He could count to a million as far as she was concerned. "The cat?"

The shampoo bubbles were running down her arms. "Still only likes the front half of mice." Sam wiped a glob of lather from her eyebrow.

"Your sister?"

"Fine." She worked hard to scrub away the filth of the holding tank. "And speaking of Sharon, why'd you have to involve her in your little plot, anyway?"

"I didn't call her. Your secretary did."

"You could have stopped her."

"And said what? 'Let's not bother telling Sharon that her sister's dead'? Why didn't you call her while you were in New York waiting for the DNA report?"

It had never occurred to her.

"I didn't realize you were a twin. No wonder your father thought he was going to the movies with her."

"Well, now you know."

"What's it like being a twin?"

"What's it like not being a twin?"

Derek took a last drag and flushed the stinking butt down the toilet. It was about time. "How's your father?"

"He's bedridden," she said as she slid under the water.

The hazel flecks in his dark eyes reflected the moving water as she came up for air. "I'm sorry, Samantha."

She wiped hers with the back of her hand. "Damn! Got soap in my eyes."

Derek grabbed a washcloth. "Look up."

She brushed his hand away. She didn't need his help. She tugged at the corner of the wet towel.

Without so much as a by-your-leave, good ol' Derek pushed his jacket sleeve above his elbows and fished through the cloudy water for the sliver of soap she'd knocked out of the tray. How had she ever taken a bath without his help?

"You know that rent-a-doc you hired from Salt Lake?"

Derek nodded as he soaped the washcloth. "Dr. Gordon."

"He's still in Sheridan. His wife's expect—"

"I'm glad. You were working too hard." Busy fingers scrubbed her toes with the washcloth. She jerked her foot away. Imbecile! "Though I doubt you've slowed down much."

"Let me have that washcloth." Sam ripped it out of his hand.

Expressionless, Derek handed over the shrinking sliver of soap. Rising, he took the hand towel and unfolded it. "Come on out and I'll try to dry you off."

"I want to soak a bit longer. Go on to bed."

Derek draped the small towel over the toilet and left.

Sam slid down into the water until she was totally submerged and couldn't feel the tears. He'd only been able to unnerve her because of everything else that day. The accumulation of one unpleasantry after another.

The hand towel wasn't sufficient, and she wished she'd not been so damned modest. She slipped the nightshirt over her damp skin, cursing Derek for making her get the big towel wet. Though shivering, she still took a moment to look at her profile in the full-length mirror behind the door. He'd have to be blind not to notice. Why didn't he say anything?

Screw him. Back ramrod-straight, she opened the door. "Shit, it's cold," she said, hurrying to the bed.

Derek held up the covers as she slipped under, then leaned over and turned off the nightstand light. "Move over this way where it's warmer." Strong arms pulled her to the hard warm body.

She nuzzled in close, shivering in his arms. "I'm so cold."

"You'll warm up soon, Samantha," he whispered as he kissed her wet, tangled hair. "You've had a rough day; try to get some sleep."

6

"ARE YOU GETTING up in earnest, or only long enough to hug the toilet bowl?"

Sam lifted the eyelid not resting on the rim of the toilet and looked up at Derek. Red-eyed, unshaven, he was not what you would call a breath of fresh air.

"Would you like me to hold your head?" Derek asked, gently bunching up her wild tangled hair and anchoring it under her shirt in back.

She felt her pyloric sphincter contract again, sending up the bitter bile. She turned her head down into the toilet and retched for the umpteenth time. She was left weak and helpless, and she wanted him to hold her head. And at the same time, she didn't want him to see her like this; it was one of those things a person would rather do in private. Besides, she was mad at him.

Derek was doing something behind her, moving around making noise. He had been fishing for the washcloth, she realized as soon as he started cleaning her face. The good-sized towel was still floating in a tub full of cloudy water.

"Do this every morning?"

Sam groaned.

"How about a Seven-Up to give you something more palatable to bring up?"

Her reply sunk to the bottom of the bowl. She was shaking noticeably.

Derek ripped the paper from one of the glasses next to the sink and filled the glass with water. "Here, drink this."

His concern was more than she could stomach. She pushed his hand away and struggled up. "I'm fine now. Really." He stood mutely scrutinizing her every movement.

"I have my doubts," he said as she retched again brushing her teeth. "Are you coming back to bed?"

Sam shook her head.

"Would you like me to order something from room service?"

Room service! Was he crazy? She was sicker than a dog and he offers her room service. She smirked at his reflection in the mirror, though it wasn't the reflection she held against him. Actually, there was nothing she liked more than being held against him. Sam was at his mercy whenever his strong arms closed around her. Not that she was about to tell him. Her eyes moved down his deeply tanned body to the line across his tight, flat belly where a very small bikini swimsuit must have been his sole protector from the sun. "That's quite an impressive tan. The spy business must have more free time than I'd imagined."

"We spies work mostly at night under the cloak of darkness." His white teeth flashed.

She retched again.

"Do you have some pills somewhere?" His eyes were filled with worry. Not that it mattered to her how he felt. "Do you want me to get some?"

"Derek, thank you for your concern, but I'm just fine—and late."

"Where are you going?"

"To the meetings, of course."

"Fine. I'll get dressed."

"You can't go," she said to his back before he disappeared. Derek returned. "And why not?"

"You're not a doctor."

"So?"

Sam looked at her toothbrush, deciding if she should chance sticking it in her mouth again. In the end she threw it into her tattered makeup bag and picked up her hairbrush. "Do you think they'd let me into one of your superspy conferences?"

He sanded the door frame with his fingertips. "I don't know. If you could find our clandestine meeting place, I suppose you'd be welcome to join up."

The brush flew from her hand as she tried to get through a tangle.

He picked it up and gave it a try. "I wish you would've called."

Sam yanked the brush back, threw it across the vanity, and gathered her hair into a ponytail. "You lost my number?"

Derek unclogged the tub, wringing water from the towel. The sucking soapy water circled the drain. "I didn't think you'd appreciate hearing from me."

"You mean after your treasonous deception?"

"Treasonous is not the word you're looking for." He wrung the yellow towel practically hard enough to make the color run.

"No, I guess not. You and your CIA buddy, Adam—"

"Adam's with the DIA, Defense Intelligence Agency. And he's not my buddy. I didn't know him from any other Adam." He threw the towel down. "I need a cigarette."

"Forgive my ignorance. We nonsuperspy types have trouble telling all the good guys apart. Let's see, he's DIA. You and your buddy Scotty are CIA. That means Adam saves the country, you and Scotty save the world." She followed him through the bedroom as he searched for his cigarettes.

"Something like that." He stuck a cigarette between his lips.

"Unless the good guys killing the bad guys in the country ask one of the supergood guys to stop saving the world long enough to help them save the country."

Derek threw an unlit match on the dresser and tore another from the book. "Sounds about right."

"Sounds like a low-budget spy movie to me. You know, the bad good-guy-spy, the good bad-guy-spy, the good guy that the spies try to do bad things to, and the good girl everyone tries to do bad things to."

"Well," he cupped the sputtering match to the tip of his cigarette, breathing in deeply, "we had most of the necessary elements. Jeffrey, the bad good-guy, yours truly, the good bad-guy, and you, the good girl we both—"

Sam struggled to open the window.

Derek balanced his cigarette on the corner of the dresser and moved to her, swooping her into his arms. "I'm sorry, Samantha." He stroked her hair as if she were a hurt child instead of a responsible grown woman. "I would have given anything to have been there for you. If only I really were a journalist—"

Sam pushed away and turned back to the window. "I was in love with you. Did you have so little faith in my love that you thought a little matter of your occupation would make a difference?"

"And my duplicity?" he asked, unlocking the window.

She slid the window up so hard it hit the top and bounced down. "I was fucking pissed off. You could have been honest with me. I would have kept your secret—I have kept your secret. There," she said once the window was open and she was able to breathe. "How did you expect us to have a decent relationship laced with lies? All you had to do was be honest."

"And you? What about your cloak-and-dagger shenani-gans? And what about now? Do you have any idea what kind of strings I had to pull to get you out of the slammer? And speaking of honesty—"

Sam stomped to the drawer and pulled out clean under-wear and everything else around it. The cigarette dropped to the floor. "What about honesty?"

He picked up the cigarette, rubbing out the hot ashes blackening the carpet. "Isn't there something you want to tell me?"

She deliberately looked away, focusing all her attention on the gold wallpaper. "Yes—this is a nonsmoking room."

"Anything else?" He took two quick drags before he disappeared into the bathroom to flush the cigarette down the toilet.

"I told the police everything I know and I'm sure you've already read the report."

"I meant of a more personal nature."

Sam heard a snap and felt the fabric give as she pulled on her pantyhose. "I just ran my fucking nylons."

Derek picked up a white egg on the floor. "I believe you'll find a new pair in here."

She ripped it out of his hand. "Thanks ever so much."

Happy Cleaner picked up the rest of her spilled belongings and folded them tidily into the drawer. "I'll walk you over."

"That will be just swell!" Sam watched him put on his pants in the manner she suspected he would, one leg at a time. "I'll show you to the hospitality room. Perhaps *Aunt June* will be there."

Derek sat on the bed next to her and shook out a sock. "Good. I want to thank her for calling. It's not every day I get to take the red-eye cross-country."

"And weren't we lucky you were in New York."

He took a deep breath and let it out slowly. "Samantha," he said in a calm, deep voice. "I'm not going to argue with you any longer. I think our purposes are better served putting our heads together instead of butting them."

"Our purposes?"

"Somehow I don't think you'll walk away from this Smith thing." He sighed. "I'll help."

Sam threw her arms around him, bulldozing him flat to the bed. "I knew there was something about you I loved."

"My stupidity?" he managed to say before she covered his lips with hers.

▽

7

"IT WAS A GOOD idea to come to the dining room instead of standing around the lobby with a cup of coffee, don't you think?" Chris bit into a heavily buttered blueberry muffin. Sam wondered if he ever tested his cholesterol levels.

"Too many ears," Sam said to Dr. Sommers, sitting next to her, "and one of those ears may have stuck Smith with a needle."

Dr. Sommers nodded. "I fear that's true, though we won't know until the toxicology reports come back."

"You were satisfied with the autopsy?" Chris asked.

Sam was sipping steaming tea.

Sommers answered. "It was thorough." He folded his arms and leaned across the table to Chris. "But I'm more interested in your venture, Newman."

Chris stopped midbite, delighted to have a willing audience. "Well, if you really want to hear."

Sam glanced beyond Sommers out the window. There should be laws against people droning on and on. She strained to see the two people by the taxi. Every nerve ending in her body prickled. She leaned closer to see, and must have caught her elbow on the side of Sommers's saucer, flipping the coffee cup over. She scarcely heard the racket and their protests, and barely felt Sommers move her paralyzed elbow. All of her senses were centered on Derek—and the young redhead whose arms were around his neck.

"Sam?" Chris turned to the window and craned his neck to see.

She was just dimly aware of Sommers wiping up the coffee spill. The couple moved and Sam had to practically crawl into Sommers's lap to see. He didn't mind, he was busy swiping at the stream of coffee.

Derek was a liar and a cheat! She pressed closer to the window as Derek helped the miniskirted woman into the taxi.

"Who's that with Derek?" Chris asked innocently.

"How kind of your husband to see the widow off," Sommers said.

"The widow?" Chris asked.

"The widow?" It was her voice.

He pointed out the window. "Mrs. Smith."

"That was Doyle Smith's widow?" Chris asked.

Sam leaned back in her chair with a sigh. Derek had vanished, anyway. Her clothes were wet. Great! She folded back the soaking tablecloth as Sommers sponged her off.

"You've met Derek?" Chris asked.

Sommers caught the waiter's attention. "We've had a little mishap here." To Chris: "I met him last night."

Sam looked over at Chris. "And just what time did he get in, this *husband* of mine?"

Chris shrugged.

"I sat in a dirty cell until after three in the morning with the strangest-looking group of women you'd never hope to meet in an entire lifetime, and Derek was in town!"

"It *was* fairly late when he came calling," Sommers said diplomatically. "We'd been back from the harbor cruise quite a while."

The cruise was from six to ten, this Sam knew from the brochure. "Let's say you were his first stop and it was at eleven, that leaves four hours. Chris?"

Chris shrugged.

Sommers looked at his watch. "Perhaps we should start back?"

Chris gulped his coffee and popped the tail end of a croissant into his mouth.

The waiter approached with a busboy and a new tablecloth.

"We need to get back to the meetings. Will you see that this gets billed to my room?" Sommers held out his key.

"Yes, sir."

Chris was long gone by the time Sam managed to get around the waiter.

8

THE WIDOW WAS still on Sam's mind when the meeting broke up for lunch. She started to pump Chris some more, but stopped when she saw Derek laughing with the two women manning the information table. The green-eyed monster sent her blood pressure soaring. She had no hold on him—he was a free agent and could flirt with whomever he chose—but his affirmation of love seemed highly questionable.

"Derek's a real lady-killer, isn't he?"

Sam scoffed at Chris. "My bite is worse than my bark. I suggest you hightail it to June before I prove it."

Chris mumbled something about pregnancy and permanent PMS, stuck his hands in his pockets, and waddled toward the staircase. Sam bit her nasty tongue and ran after him. "Chris." She felt a hand on her arm.

"Ready for lunch?"

She watched as Chris's shiny crown disappeared down the stairs. She would apologize later. She turned to Derek. "I'm not hungry. I need to go over to the morgue and see if the preliminary toxicology reports are in."

"After lunch."

"I have meetings after lunch." Sam pulled the cutesy teddy-bear smock away from her apple-shaped body and pointed to the humongous coffee stain. "I did this when you were busy kissing Mrs. Smith." She hated the maternity clothes the radiologist's wife had loaned her; she wanted in the worst way to wear her denim jumper.

Derek took her elbow and led her to the staircase. "When Mrs. Smith was kissing me, to be precise."

A secure person would not be jealous. "I understand you made the rounds before bailing me out."

"I needed to know what was what. How much trouble could you get into in a cell?" She stopped to ponder. He squeezed the flesh above her elbow. "If I buy lunch, will you forgive me?"

That irresistible boyish charm was in his voice. "It depends on the lunch."

"I have it on reliable source that we *have* to eat fresh seafood at the Brigantine." He leaned over and brushed the top of her head with his lips. He'd kissed every square inch of it by time they'd descended the stairs. She hated the way he made her feel.

"The Brigantine sounds fine." She smiled up as she slipped through the door Derek held open. "As soon as I change."

Derek caught her arm and pointed her in the opposite direction. "You can change after lunch. This way."

Sam dug in her heels. He was so irritating, and her nerves were frazzled. "Bad enough I had to sit through the lecture, I'm not going to lunch looking like this."

"Our room's not ready yet."

"We're still sharing mine?"

Derek pointed to a flower. "Bird of Paradise. Isn't it lovely?"

Sam bent over to feel the delicate orange and purple petals, getting a tiny thump in the ribs for her trouble. Sam pressed the pod open to see how many petals were still inside. It was lovely, but his ploy to avoid the question hadn't worked. "Did you forget the question, Derek?"

"We've moved."

"You took the liberty of moving me?" Her voice was not altogether serene, she suspected.

"Yours was a nonsmoking room. We're taking one with a balcony." Derek ran a tender hand over her cheek. "I'll smoke outside." He lifted her chin and gave her a lingering kiss. She forgot her purpose.

They fell into blissful silence and walked hand-in-hand across Orange Avenue. Blissful, that is, until Derek jerked her out of the path of a fast-moving sports car. "Did you see that?"

Derek coaxed her forward. "Drives as fast as you, Samantha."

"I don't drive like that down a main drag."

He bent over and kissed the tip of her nose. "I like your nose the way it is. Don't be saying things to make it grow." Using that criteria, hers could never be as long as his. "This is it."

The fishy smell was awful. "Derek, I can't eat here. The smell is making me ill."

"Just a minute." He walked to the bar and took a couple of matchbooks out of a wicker basket on the counter. He said something that made the cocktail waitress smile. Sam decided to wait for him on the street.

"Sorry. Bad idea." Derek pocketed the matches and took her hand. "Where to?"

She looked around for another restaurant. "Doesn't look like there is anything. Maybe we could go to our room and call Domino's?"

"Our room's not ready." He pointed across the busy street they'd just taken life in hand to cross. "There's a Wendy's in that little mall."

She saw the little mall, but not the Wendy's sign; she'd take it on faith. She liked Wendy's and every other fast-food place they had in Sheridan. No fuss, no bother, and no lost time.

Times were bad. Only five or six businesses were leasing in the small mall; the other two-thirds were boarded up. A blond in the jewelry store was setting a pearl necklace into the window. She did that passably, but spilled a great deal of cleavage over the top of her black jersey dress. That didn't bother Sam half as much as the way she smiled at Derek— like they were old friends. What bothered her most was the shocked look the woman gave her, and Sam knew it wasn't because of the coffee-stained top. She wanted to die of embarrassment. If Derek wasn't going to mention the baby, neither was she.

"Downstairs," Derek said, pulling her under his arm.

He led her to an out-of-the-way table. "What's your pleasure, ma'am?" She'd forgotten that English butler routine of his.

"A Single and a Diet Coke."

Even the cute little Oriental girl behind the counter treated him like her long-lost cousin. When he was back with the order, Sam asked, "Was your picture in today's newspaper, or something?"

"I hope not. Why?"

"Everyone seems to know you."

"Probably because they do. I was here earlier." He doled out the food.

The food tasted like cardboard.

"Still feeling under the weather?" Derek wiped his mouth.

Under the weather? That was rich! "What did you learn from Mrs. Smith?"

"That she doesn't smoke." He took out a page of a computer printout and unfolded it.

"What's that?"

"Linda's convention roster." He turned it around and pointed to her name. "Samantha Turner, M.D., pathologist, Sheridan, Wyoming. And under the fee column, three hundred and sixty-five."

"Who's Linda?"

"You remember Linda? You certainly gave her a good looking-over when you saw me talking to her at the convention desk." He reached across the table and took her hand. "It's you I love, Samantha."

Sam tried to speak, but her tongue was too thick. He gave her hand a squeeze and released it. He returned to the printout.

"Here's one. Alan Martin, M.D., ob-gyn, Los Angeles, CA, seventy-five."

"What about it?"

"A gynecologist at a medical examiners' convention? Seventy-five in the fee column must be one day's worth." He continued to peruse the printout. "Why does your denim jumper reek of Mrs. Smith's perfume?"

"How did you know the perfume on my jumper was hers?"

"Anyone who has ever walked into La Fleuri Parfum Salon in Paris remembers the scent. Why did you straighten up the Smith room?"

Sam shrugged. "It seemed like a good idea at the time. A bellman took us up. I thought they might put two and two together if Mrs. Smith told the authorities that someone had trashed the room."

He looked at her a very long and uncomfortable time. "Here's another one," he said, turning to the printout for her to see. "Nguyen Ho, D.O., pathologist, Wildomyer, CA, seventy-five." He folded the printout and stuck it in his pocket. "Aren't you going to eat?"

She tried to take a few bites. "Maybe Mrs. Smith and I have the same taste in perfume. Did you think about that?"

"You have to buy it in Paris. You ate like a bird." He gathered up their trash. "A walk on the beach is next on our agenda."

They walked slowly along the soft sand. Derek barefoot, Sam in stocking feet. She had wet-sand static cling practically to her knees. She studied the microcosm of the sand flies jumping from tiny bubbling holes in the sand.

"I could never tire of this," Derek said, breathing in the fresh sea air noisily. He pulled the rubber band from around her ponytail, letting her hair fall over her shoulders.

"We never did."

"You and Dad . . . I'd forgotten you had a place on the beach."

Memories rode the waves. "A lifetime ago." She felt an arm glide tenderly across her shoulders.

"Think I'm getting like my dad." Sam stuffed her shoes in her bag, mainly to have a chance to brush away a runaway tear. "I can't remember John's face anymore."

"Nothing's wrong with that steel-trap mind of yours. Time has a way of doing that to all of us . . . What's important is that you remember what he was inside."

Sam nodded, keeping her eyes seaward.

Derek pointed to a surfer riding a plunging breaker. They watched as the half-cylinder toppled and crashed around the boy in a thunderous roar.

Derek fished for a cigarette.

"Still have the ashtray?" It was a gentle reminder.

He cupped a match to the end of the cigarette. "The one with a piece of lung tissue at the base?" Derek nodded as he shook out the flame. "Used it since you gave it to me last Christmas and the lung doesn't look any worse."

Sam punched him in the ribs. "That's because it's under glass. And it was bad enough to kill its previous owner, for your information."

When the cigarette was nothing more than a butt, he threw it into the water. Sam looked disapprovingly up at him.

"You're making me feel guilty for wanting to smoke."

"Good."

The hotel was just a dot on the horizon when Derek placed his Topsiders on a large boulder. He swept her off her feet and set her gently on the rock beside his shoes. "I bought you something this morning." He brought out a jeweler's ring box and placed it in the palm of her hand.

The velvety case felt like fire. He could surely see her hand shake, hear her pounding heart. She didn't know how she felt about Derek or what she wanted to be to him—but to his family she'd never be anything more than the wicked stepmother. She gave him back the box. "I can't accept it."

"Samantha, why do you have to make everything so complicated?" He opened the box and took out a hefty diamond solitaire. "I could have gotten this for a fraction of the cost in Bangkok only a few days ago, had I known."

"That has a ring of chauvinism."

"Practicality." He dropped to his knees and held out the ring. "Please marry me, Samantha."

"Don't." She looked around at the other people on the beach. Two kids were openly watching; their mothers were slightly more discreet with their glances. "You're embarrassing me."

Derek ran a finger over John's ring on her left hand and then slipped his ring onto her right ring finger. He brushed the hair the wind had blown wild away from her eyes. "I love you, Samantha, and I want you to be my wife." She slid from the rock and tried to run. Derek caught her and twirled her around. "Give me one good reason."

She looked down at the rings. "Because I'm pregnant."

"Samantha, where I come from, that's a good reason to marry."

"And what if it's Jeffrey's?"

He lifted her chin. "A parent is someone who walks the floors with a sick baby during the wee hours of the night, is there to kiss a skinned knee, to go to baseball practice, or a dance recital." He hugged her tightly. "I want to be that someone."

Tears misted her eyes. "And your mother and sisters?"

"You're marrying me, not them. And if they can't accept you, that's their loss. And I'll always be your companion."

"Your father said about the same thing. That I was marrying him, not his family." Pushing away, she looked beyond the ocean to the horizon. "But the alienation embittered him in time."

Derek tightened his hold. "Alienation from his children. Isn't that what you would be doing to me if you *didn't* marry me?"

"If the baby's yours." Sam buried her face in his shirt. She couldn't hold back the tears any longer.

Derek stroked the back of her hair as she let it rip. She hadn't had a full blowout like this since she didn't know when.

"Honey, in a minute we're going to be underwater." He

tucked a lock of hair behind her ear. "Anyone who is half you is worth loving. It really isn't important to me whether the baby is biologically mine or not. I'll love him or her the same."

She curled her toes into the wet sand as a wave splashed to her hem. "But where would we live?" A sob caught in her throat. "I have a practice in Sheridan."

"We'll live at the ranch or wherever you want."

"What would you do in Sheridan?"

"This is it." He swooped her up just as the water crashed into them. He had taken the brunt of the wave, pretending it was nothing. She put her arms around his neck, luxuriating in being carried. She felt a slight longing as he gave her back her feet on dry sand. "I'll take care of the kids."

"Kids? As in plural?"

Derek put a hand on her middle. "Everyone should have the opportunity to fight with a sibling. We don't want our firstborn to be deprived, do we?"

"We're a bit old for this."

The yellow flecks in his eyes danced with amusement. "You're a little old, anyway. I'm still considered a great catch." He picked up their things. "I promise to be the prime caretaker. Their pictures can be on my passports. Passport."

"And just how many passports do we have?"

He shrugged. "Derek Turner has but one."

Which was one more than Samantha Turner had. "That's rather an evasive answer."

"But true."

"And probably misleading." To his silence, she said, "All right. We'll have as many as you like, as long as you're the one—" the rest of the sentence and a shriek were swept away with the wave.

Their clothes were plastered to their bodies. "Now it's time to change." Derek laughed as he grabbed her wet hand. It was the first time she'd seen him laugh.

▽

9

"LET ME GUESS," Sam said with the witticism of a fire-breathing dragon as the elevator stopped on the sixth floor of the tower building. "Six six two nine?"

"The hotel's full and it *is* an ocean-view room," Derek said evenly. "You didn't want me to have to look at the parking lot while blowing smoke out the window, did you?"

"You're not making me feel guilty. You're the one who should—" Sam left the thought hanging as they turned the corridor and saw the cleaning lady standing beside her cart in front of their door.

Derek reached out and slipped the Do Not Disturb card off the handle. "Could you give us just a moment to change out of these wet clothes? Then it's all yours."

She pinched up her face. "This is the last room. I'm supposed to get off in half an hour."

Derek gave the woman his flashiest smile. "I'm truly sorry for the inconvenience." He tucked a twenty into her hand. He needn't have bothered. It was obvious that he'd already charmed her out of her socks.

"It's no inconvenience at all."

Derek ushered Sam into the room. "Is there a woman alive you can't—" Her question died as she looked at a man in a suit crawling on his hands and knees, flicking a little paintbrush against the base of the closet door.

"It's all right, Samantha," Derek said as he put his hands on her shoulders to keep her from jumping out of her skin. "You're not finished, yet?"

"Almost."

Now that she was getting a good look, the whole place had been dusted with magnetic ferric oxide. They put the Sheridan police to shame. Sheridan's idea of lifting prints was to put a little oxide on the doorknobs and around the light switches.

"The maid's chomping at the bit."

"Tell us about it," a man in shirtsleeves called, stepping out of the tub. "Ma'am."

"Find anything?" Derek asked.

The spy-type at the closet shook his head. "Not sure yet."

"Found one of Dr. Turner's prints in the corner under the vanity."

Derek looked questioningly at her.

"The perfume."

"Of course." Derek slipped his hand into his left pants pocket and pulled out a matchbook. "Where's a bag?"

"On the dresser."

Sam followed him through the room. "Who are they?" she whispered. "That's one of the matchbooks you got at that place that smelled so . . . fishy." Even the memory of the smell turned her stomach. "You think someone over there is connected with Smith's murder?"

"No." He zipped the matchbook into the plastic bag, then stuck his hand in his other pocket. "These are the matches you saw me pick up. This is the book I took from the table over there when I first spoke with Tiffany . . . Mrs. Smith."

Sam understood about the matches, but couldn't help belaboring one small point. *"Tiffany?"*

"She declined one of my cigarettes, saying she didn't smoke." He moved easily over the undercurrent as if he'd had plenty of practice. "Your David Sommers assured me that Dr. Smith's lungs, unlike mine, would never be used as an ashtray decoration."

Sam let the opportunity slip away in order to concentrate on Tiffany. "I think the subject was Tiffany."

"She doesn't smoke."

"So you said. Perhaps the Smiths collect matches from the different places they've been?"

He picked up the bag. "These were used." Derek lifted her suitcase to the unmade bed and popped it open. "Everything you own now has a La Fleuri scent."

"I'll be so spoiled, I won't give the Avon lady the time of day," she said, watching him take out her khaki safari shift. He looked disapprovingly at the ragged edge on one of the belt loops she'd cut off just before leaving Sheridan.

"When next we're in Paris, I'll buy you your own bottle." He handed her appropriate underwear, and then fished through his pockets. He clipped the belt loop close to the seam with his trusty Swiss Army knife. Those Eagle Scouts.

"Like I have time to gallivant all over the world."

He handed over the dress. "Well, when the children and I are in Paris, we'll bring you back a bottle."

"Thanks."

"Come on. Let's see if we can talk Dennis into letting you use the bathroom." Derek whispered in her ear. "Put a finger print on the light fixture. He'll love it."

▽

10

DEREK LEFT SAMANTHA with her marching orders: after the afternoon conference session, she was to rest up for the evening's Mexico excursion. He left Uncle Chris orders: he was to make sure Samantha didn't leave the hotel grounds. He left Aunt June orders: she was to keep an eye on the wayward pair. Still, he hoped his visit to Alan Martin, M.D., wouldn't take long.

There was something in the way Samantha had raised the question about the address of the rental car agency. In the back of his mind he envisioned Samantha off somewhere instead of resting in their room. And the last thing he wanted was for her to get behind the steering wheel of a car.

He was torn between keeping an eye on Samantha and making this trip so that she wouldn't. He frankly couldn't have cared less who murdered Doyle Smith. But Samantha was involved and she had a peculiar penchant for falling into trouble.

Derek reminded himself that her little visit to the holding tank had given him his opportunity. She had never been far from his thoughts since that mess in Sheridan, but now she was all he could think about. What if Aunt June hadn't called? He might never have seen her again. He had gone ahead and written the feature story on her buffalo, hoping for a call or a note from her. But nothing. And now he understood why.

The mere thought of being a husband and father would have unnerved him in his pre-Samantha days. Now, he was almost looking forward to it. A little time to get used to the idea was all he needed. Marrying Samantha was going to go over in a big way with his sisters and mother.

Traffic northbound on 405 was not as bad as expected. Two hours after renting the car and leaving San Diego he found Dr. Martin's abortion clinic in the middle of a seedy neighborhood. Street people wandered aimlessly, gangbangers patrolled the streets in low-slung gas-guzzlers, and black children sold crack to shaking junkies. Juxtaposed were militant right-to-life protesters and a row of bored police.

Derek parked between a late-model Jaguar and a patrol car. He left the glove compartment open to show that he had nothing worth stealing, paid the meter, and made his way into the storefront clinic without interference from either faction. The door clanged shut hard enough to get the devil's attention, but not that of the two women behind the reception desk.

The waiting area had two occupants, a white girl who appeared to be in her very early teens and a young woman Derek took for the girl's mother. He waited for the middle-aged biddies to stop working each other up over the new nurse's preferential treatment. When he had their full attention, he gave them the smile he reserved for the most disagreeable. The scowl on the nearest woman disappeared. She sprang up.

"Can I help you?"

"I sure hope so. I wonder if I might see your Dr. Martin for a moment."

Dr. Martin, he was assured, was too busy to take the time to speak to him. But in the end, the secretary arranged the briefest of meetings after he produced his journalism credentials and swore his visit had nothing to do with his job, that it was strictly personal.

Secretaries ran the world. The one running the office disappeared behind doors. She returned with a smile and ushered Derek in.

"Would you care for a cup of coffee?" the carrot-topped,

frecklefaced young doctor asked as he poured half a cup for himself.

Derek pulled out a dilapidated chair and sat at the folding table. "No thanks."

The doctor slumped in the chair across from Derek. He seemed to be shouldering a mountain of fatigue, but with protesters at his door, that was understandable.

"I'm afraid I've wasted your time, doctor."

"Oh?" he asked as he put the steaming coffee to his lips.

"I'm looking for another Alan Martin—a buddy from Vietnam."

Dr. Martin smiled, showing a boyish grin and uneven teeth. "Guess so, I was just a kid when it ended."

"We were all just kids, but we had to grow up fast." Derek hauled out his cigarettes. "Do you mind?"

Martin gave him a hesitant shake. His Samantha wouldn't have been as polite. Derek held out the pack to him. "No, thanks. I don't smoke," the good doctor said, "but go ahead."

"My wife is attending a medical examiners' conference in San Diego. When I saw your name on the list I had hoped you might be my Alan Martin." Derek took a long drag and blew out three smoke rings. Dr. Martin looked on appreciatively. "I looked for you today, but they said you were only there for one day."

"I wouldn't have made even that if I hadn't been desperate for the continuing education credit. A medical examiners' conference isn't at all useful to my field, but San Diego is close and it was my day off."

"A pity to waste your day off like that."

"Actually, I was there only long enough to sign in. My wife and son were in the car. We went to the zoo." He drained the cup and pitched it into the trash as he got up. "Well, I need to get back to work. I hope you find your Alan Martin."

Derek got to his feet. "Thank you."

The trip had been a waste of time.

▽

11

"Sam, Derek said you weren't to go anywhere."

"Oh, shut up, Chris, and buckle up."

"June'll tell Derek."

"Yeah, she's turned out to be a regular tattletale." Sam flung the map at Chris. "Follow the red line the rental guy drew to Wildomyer—make sure I don't take any wrong turns."

Wildomyer, a sleepy desert community some eighty miles northeast of San Diego, was a developer's paradise. Sam and Chris left the rental car in a blacktop parking lot between the three-story hospital and the doctors' offices addition under construction and made their way toward the Inland Valley Hospital.

Everything in the medical center was new. The padded plastic wallpaper smelled fresh and the maroon carpet showed no signs of wear. The dark stripe in the wallpaper reminded her more of a new prison than a hospital, though graffiti covered the walls of the jail cell she had been left to rot in.

"I'm going to the rest room, Chris. Be right back."

By the time she got back, Chris was enchanting the ancient volunteer behind the information desk. Her hospital-issue pink jacket was the only thing new about her.

"She's finding Nguyen Ho for us."

A sign pointing to Pathology would have sufficed. But the woman's eyes were enlivened from being needed. Her hand wiggled down the list. "I don't see him listed."

"He's not one of your doctors?" Sam asked.

"Oh . . . the doctor list. I thought you meant patient."
The elderly volunteer found the list—pressed between two
sheets of permatizing plastic to insure newness—and metic-
ulously started working her way down.

"Actually," Sam said, "if you'll just point us toward
Pathology."

"Pathology?"

"The blood lab," Chris allowed.

A gnarled finger pointed down the main hall. "To the left
at the first intersection."

"Thanks," Sam said as she pulled Chris along.

"I mean second," the woman called.

Sam gave a wave to tell the woman that they got it. The
lab, though smaller than the one she and Sommers visited
in San Diego, was state-of-the-art. She was beginning to feel
like the poor cousin.

"Dr. Newman!" An Asian man pushed away from his
microscope and rushed over. "Doctor Newman, this is an
honor. I have read all of your papers." Chris postured as he
shook the man's outstretched hand. Sam had thought of
Chris as a friend for so long that she had forgotten his
standing in the medical community.

"Dr. Ho?" Chris asked.

"Yes, I am Ho." The doctors pumped hands some more.

"Dr. Ho, I'd like to introduce Dr. Turner."

Sam smiled. "Hello."

Doctor Ho studied her. "Dr. Turner. Dr. Turner. That rings
a bell." He shook his head. "No, it was John Turner."

"What was John Turner?"

"A brilliant paper on autoimmune hemolytic anemia."

Sam and Chris exchanged knowing glances. It had been
her study as a resident; John had sponsored the paper, since
he was a member of the academy and she was a lowly
resident. John had added the brilliance.

"Dr. Turner and I were in the neighborhood and thought
we'd stop by." Chris gave Dr. Ho a wink. "A busman's
holiday, you might say."

Sam walked over to the work area Ho had occupied before they interrupted. She looked longingly at his state-of-the-art Nikon binocular microscope. She used to have one, though not this fancy.

"How very kind of you. I only wish now that I had extended an invitation following your toxicology lecture. I had no idea."

Sam hurried back to them. "You heard Dr. Newman speak at the medical examiners' convention?"

"Yes, a very good lecture."

That was very bad. "Were you there the next day?"

He shook his head. "I could arrange to be gone only the one day."

Sam caught Chris's eye. It was time to leave.

$\triangledown$

12

"You LOOK A little green, Samantha, you all right?"

Sam's nails dug deeper into the time-crackled vinyl on the bus's armrests. "Just fine, Derek." Stupid questions deserved stupid answers.

"You did manage to rest this afternoon, didn't you?"

She had raced back to San Diego and managed to get out of her clothes and into bed before he waltzed in. "Of course I did." He would be none the wiser if blabbermouth June kept it zipped. Derek had already told her that his trip was a waste of time; she had to figure out a way to save him another one to Ho. "Oh, and by the way." She leaned over and whispered in his ear. "That doctor from Wildomyer was at the conference the first day, not the day Doyle Smith died."

"How do you know that?"

"He spoke to Chris." It was sort of true.

Derek sighed. "Fix your eyes on the carrier, honey." He patted her hand solicitously. "It should help the motion sickness."

"What carrier?" Sam asked, looking out at the blue ocean.

He turned her head. "There. Can't you see the fleet? It's dotting the entire horizon."

At last she saw the silver sliver, which seemed smaller than the child's small boat that had poured out of her cereal box a few weeks before. She fastened her eyes on the peppered horizon as the chartered bus drove south on the sandbar joining Coronado and Mexico. Why had she come? She knew the answer. Like every other woman, Sam fell victim to

Derek's charm. Chris had been unable to persuade her to sign up for the Tijuana tour, but when Derek insisted they use the tickets *Tiffany* left behind on the dresser . . . well, she was here, wasn't she? It would be their chance to find out if any other doctors had departed prematurely, he had insisted just before he gave her a lingering kiss. Logic played no part in her decision to accompany him.

The bus nosed down the isthmus at a snail's pace. Heavy road construction. Wave upon wave of nausea surged through her as the stiffly sprung coach crossed a series of ruts. Sam squinted through the white flash of the slanting sun on the dusty window in order to keep her eyes riveted on the shimmering ship—for all the good it did. As time wore on, Sam's eyes wandered to the soft swirling sand twisting at the road's shoulder and to the lazy waves nipping at the white sand.

The bus left the picturesque coastline for the freeway and its jammed rush-hour traffic. The stop-and-go was doing her in.

"I wish I could do something for you," Derek whispered in her ear.

Sam managed a smile. The ugliness so typically fringing large cities became more noticeable south of the border. The lean-tos slapped together with scraps of plywood were the good ones; many homes in the low-rent district looked like dilapidated cardboard boxes. Tall weeds were littered with trash, broken concrete, and broken-down vehicles. Roaming dogs and dirty children were everywhere.

"How can people live like this?"

"Haven't you ever been here before?"

"No."

Derek patted her hand. "Then I'm glad we came. It'll make you appreciate the U.S. Spend six weeks in the Yucatan and you'll think this part of Mexico is paradise."

"How could anything be worse than this?"

"Mayans fight a constant battle to keep the jungle from reclaiming the land."

The crumbling buildings in town seemed like palaces by

comparison to what they had passed, but their ugliness, too, loomed out at her. At a corner, a young girl stood laughing with an army guard. "Look, Derek, he has a gun over his shoulder."

Derek whispered, "An AK-47. Welcome to the other world."

Being out in the other world was worse than driving through it. Vendors yelled at her in broken English and shoved their wares in her face.

It was a mystery to Sam why June seemed to be having the time of her life. June pushed her glasses up the bridge of her thin nose, magnifying her eyes until they bugged out like a cartoon character. Bless her heart. "I used to love spending hours bartering with the street vendors"—June lifted her skirt to show Derek her scarred knees—"before my buggered-up knees made me a prime candidate for a convalescent home."

"Now, Aunt June," Derek said with a gentle smile, "you and I both know that it'd take more than a little knee surgery to slow you down."

"You look a sight better than our Sam here, at any rate," Chris said, with no compunction whatsoever about butting in. "June used to tell me how much money she'd saved me at sales. I never could get her to understand that she could save me even more money if she didn't go shopping at all."

A bent woman touched Sam's arm, saying something Sam didn't understand. It took a moment to realize that the woman was young, aged by hardship, not years. The elder of the two children at the wafer-thin woman's side held out a crusty jar.

"She wants money for milk," June explained.

Sam's guilt was overwhelming. She had so much and this poor woman had nothing. She turned to Derek. "Will you lend me some Mexican money?"

Derek took a dollar and stuffed it into the jar. He roughed up the boy's hair as he said, "Vaya con Dios."

The mother took his hand and spoke lovingly. Sam

understood the emotion, if not the words. Derek squeezed the woman's hand. "De nada."

Sam turned to watch them go. They held the jar out to the next tourist, who brushed them off with harsh words. "You gave her an American dollar."

"She'll sell it at a premium. It's stable, the peso does nothing but decline."

Sam drew a twenty out of her purse and ran after the woman. For the first time since they left the hotel she felt good.

"Nothing like an authentic Mexican dinner," Chris exclaimed as they stood by the fountain in front of the pink stucco jai alai fronton where the doctor's group was to meet at eight.

Derek and Chris were both burdened with packages. With Derek's help as translator, June had gotten everything at bottom dollar; Sam paid whatever the vendors were asking. Derek tried to intervene, but she snapped at him, saying they had little enough. He tried buying her a multicolored rebozo, but she bought a beige one for twice the price. Draped over her shoulder, it was very concealing. He bought the Panama hat she was wearing at a tilt. She had a knife for Emil and a gob of silver bracelets tucked inside her purse. Derek said he'd take care of the knife before they went through Customs. Whatever that meant.

"Chris, whatever happened to my Nikon binocular microscope?"

"Don't know." Chris shifted under the weight of June's treasures. "Why?"

She shrugged. "Just wondered."

Derek set down two huge ceramic piggy banks Sam had bought for Lindsey and Amy, her special five-year-old girlfriends. She wouldn't have bought one for Amy, who was living with Karen's parents up in Wisconsin these days, had she been thinking clearly. Sam couldn't think of Karen's death without great regret. She'd have to mail her pig.

Every few minutes since she bought the pigs, Derek had grumbled something about not knowing how they were going to get them back to Sheridan. Now he sat on the fountain ledge and fished through his pockets for cigarettes. "Hungry?"

"I don't know about her," Chris said, "but I am. They have the best baked cheese in the world. Nothing's tastier than a nice crusted layer of goat's cheese spread on a warm tortilla."

Sam swallowed hard. Derek gathered up her hair and pulled it out from under the rebozo. "They have other things on their menu."

Chris stared at Sam. "You look awful."

Sam swallowed again. "I'm fine . . . really."

June took off her new straw hat and ran fingers through her lank metallic-brown hair. "I'm not the doctor in the family, but I don't think it's normal for you to be this sick still."

"Tell that to my body, not me."

Chris shifted his bundles. "You work too damn hard, if you ask me."

"Which no one did, you old goat!"

Chris cocked his thumb at her. "*Now* she sounds like her old self."

June shot him a warning look. With her big eyes, it was meaningful. "Still, Sam, I think you should talk to your doctor when you get back."

Derek blew smoke over his head. "Who are you seeing, Samantha?" What he was really saying was, "Now that you've ruined Amy's father's practice, not to mention his life, who are you seeing?"

"Patrick O'Neil. I don't think you met him."

The conversation ran out of steam, no one finding anything worth expressing. Derek stomped out his cigarette. "Why don't we go on in?"

The restaurant boasted an old-records motif; forty-fives hung on colored yarn from every conceivable inch of ceiling. Derek had to duck several times as they followed the waiter to the long table reserved for their group. He inched the fat pigs under the table, where Sam suspected he'd just as soon leave them permanently. "Now don't kick Lindsey's pig, Samantha. It's by your left foot."

She looked under the table and saw a curly black tail and two white cheeks. "If you'd turned it the other way I could have fed him my goat cheese."

He leaned down and reversed the pig. "Uncle Chris won't be dropping crumbs."

Chris pretended to look under the table. "Don't feed him the refried beans, Sam."

June gave him a nudge. "Show a little class."

Chris held his open palms recordward. "Didn't realize we were at a five-star restaurant. My apologies."

"Do you want to hear something truly amazing, Aunt June?" It was a rhetorical question; Derek didn't give her time to answer. "Do you know that there are two Samantha Turners from Sheridan, Wyoming?"

Sam didn't know what he was driving at, but from his tone, she didn't think she was going to like it.

They noticed, too. June fiddled with her wristwatch. Chris looked sheepishly around.

Derek went on with the subtlety of a coiled rattler. "When I returned the rental car the nice lady pulled the wrong contract and guess whose name—"

"So Chris and I went to Wildomyer to have a chat with Dr. Ho. He wasn't at the conference the day Smith died. End of story."

Derek looked at her hard.

The air was thick with silence and it stayed that way until Sam spoke again. "What exactly is jai alai?" Before anyone could explain the game—and help cut the tension—the rest of their party arrived.

Derek waved them over, the table quickly filling up. He saved the seat next to him for Linda.

"Did you remember the baked cheese?" Chris asked after Derek had ordered drinks.

"I did." He turned to Linda. "Looks like most of the group is here," he said, motioning to the people settling in around the table. "I'm glad for the cancellation."

Linda lowered her eyes. "I'm only sorry about the circumstances."

"I'm certain Dr. Smith's death was very hard on you, though surely others have left for one reason or another."

"Not so far. I hate it when they do. It's murder trying to figure out the refunds."

"None?"

"Not that I'm aware of."

"Para ti," the waiter said as he set a Coke in front of Sam.

Derek sat back and lifted his beer. He didn't seem any happier.

Crisp fabric crinkled as a pretty Mexican girl brought out their combination dinners, brushing her full skirt of rainbow satin ribbons against them.

Sam picked at her food; Chris ate a colossal portion and asked for seconds.

As they headed into the fronton, Derek put down the white pig and pulled Sam into the corner. He ran a tickling finger down the line of her neck. A great glow of love and tenderness danced in his eyes. "God, I've missed you."

He stirred feelings she'd tried so hard to suppress. "I'm forgiven?"

Derek put down the other pig and pulled her tight to him, her hat tumbling to the floor. A deep kiss was all the answer she needed. He retrieved the hat and adjusted it just so. "Did anyone ever tell you you wear a hat well?" She felt a spasm hit her square in her midriff, and knew, this time, it had nothing to do with the baby. He picked up the pigs and motioned her ahead.

$\triangledown$

13

"THANK YOU FOR taking me to Mexico," Sam said as she tossed her hat on the bed.

Derek stuck the pigs in the corner of the room, out of the way if not out of mind. "I'm happy it was so . . . profitable for you."

She dropped the rebozo to the floor. She couldn't remember the last time she felt this good. "What was it called again?"

"Jai alai?" Derek took a crumpled pack of cigarettes from his jacket.

"No. The thing I won." Sam stepped out of one shoe and kicked the other across the room. Life was so wonderful.

"Exacta."

"That was amazing, huh?"

"Amazing? Amazing that you won three hundred seventy-eight dollars and forty-seven cents by betting on the colors of the players' shirts? Green and red!" He didn't sound happy at all.

"Why are you so upset? My winning got the guys loosened up and got them talking about Doyle's death."

"We didn't learn anything, did we? While they, on the other hand, learned that you have more than an academic interest in the case. One of them may have been the killer." Sam watched him disappear behind the curtains into the dark night. She hadn't said much, just that she had helped with the CPR. He was blowing it way out of proportion. She followed him onto the balcony and stood silently behind his chair, listening to the breaking waves somewhere in the darkness. How many times had she heard the familiar slapping of the waves as she and John sat on their patio in Half Moon Bay? And on windy Wyoming nights, she could hear them still. The sound stirred more memories than she cared to remember.

Derek broke the silence. "The fleet's getting closer. We'll have a nice view of them in the morning."

She took a couple of steps to the rail and peered out, seeing nothing. "How can you tell?"

"Can't you hear them?"

Sam strained against the gentle breeze and the crashing water but heard nothing else. She sensed Derek's movement behind her and heard the ashtray slide across the concrete under the chair, then felt his hand reach out and gently pull her into his lap. Strong arms folded around her.

"Tired?" he asked.

"No."

Derek swept her wind-blown hair away from her face. "Tomorrow's your wedding day, maybe we should get a little sleep."

"Tomorrow?" She struggled to get up, but his hold was too strong. "Why tomorrow?"

"Because today's gone." His voice was soft and tender. "And because I want to be married in California."

"Why?"

"Let's talk inside," Derek said as he freed her. Inside he picked up one of her shoes, then the other. "These heels are too high. Wear lower ones until the baby comes."

"Is that an order?" Sam slammed the dresser drawer on the static-charged lingerie trailing her nightshirt.

Derek placed her shoes on top of the dresser and opened the drawer to push the clothing back inside. "Under California law the mother's husband is the legal father of any child born during that union. Perhaps it's the same in Wyoming, but with Jeffrey being in Wyoming and knowing Wyoming law better than I . . . I'd just as soon we didn't chance it."

Didn't he know shoes didn't belong on top of dressers? Sam sat on the bed, her hands absently stretching the 49ers nightshirt, too tired to throw the shoes across the room. "The last time I was married in California there was a three-day waiting period. I've got to be in Sheridan before that."

Derek moved to her side and gently tucked a lock of hair behind her ear. "It's for the lab results. Lab tests can be waived if we acknowledge a sexual relationship of six months or longer." He moved a hand lightly over the fluttering baby. "No one would question that."

No question about that. Sam stormed into the bathroom, closed and locked the door. Where did he get off making unilateral decisions? She ran a hand under the tap to test the temperature of the bath water. Tomorrow! She needed more time. This could be the biggest mistake in her life. Was she really willing to have John's ex-wife as a mother-in-law? Not to mention her child's grandmother! How did she know she really loved Derek?

She did a lot of soul-searching as she soaked in the tub. And like her temperament, the water had cooled by the time she got out. She also managed to get John's ring off her swollen finger. She tucked it in the corner of her cosmetic bag for safekeeping.

Derek was on the balcony. "Derek?"

"It's chilly. Why don't you crawl into bed?" It was more a command than a question. "I'll be in in a minute."

"The conference ends at noon tomorrow. We can get the license after that."

He lifted her and carried her back inside. "The day isn't a complete loss, it seems."

"I am sorry about Dr. Ho and your Dr. Martin," she said as he lowered her gently to the bed. "Nguyen Ho simply wasn't there."

"Nor was the frecklefaced kid."

"Wait a minute." She sat up. "Does he have red hair?"

"You know him?"

"He asked what Doyle whispered to me."

$\triangledown$

14

DEREK HAD GONE to the airport and rented a Seville sometime during the night. They had left the hotel before dawn and had stayed ahead of rush-hour traffic until now. They were north of Disneyland signs, that was about all Sam knew.

"How much farther?" she asked as she looked at the sea of red tail lights ahead of them.

"Ten, twenty miles." He glanced over. "You have the map."

"Right."

"You look sick," Derek said as he inched the car forward.

She gave him a weak smile, tipped her head back against the soft leather, and looked out the passenger window at a wrecker parked on the shoulder like a vulture waiting for a road-kill special. "Hope Chris signs my name to the attendance list. If he remembers my call at all, it'll be as a bad dream."

"When he doesn't see you, he'll know to sign you in." Derek took the map out of her hand and propped it against the steering wheel.

Sam found a button that tilted her back until she could barely see over the dashboard. This stop-and-go traffic was killing her.

"We'll get off and have some breakfast." He nosed into the lane to their right.

"How am I going to ID Alan Martin if he's already inside the clinic?"

"Let's take care of you first. We'll think—"

"Oh, I see, breakfast is for me!" Her hand waved in dismissal.

He pushed the dash lighter in and brought out a pack of Camels. When the lighter popped out, Derek ignored it.

The gesture wasn't lost on Sam. She reminded herself that Derek hadn't slept six hours total in the last two nights. Although this murder business was right up his alley, he was probably more nervous than she about their impending trip to the altar. He'd managed to duck the bullet for thirty-seven years. And, unlike Derek, she'd had six months to get used to the idea of having a baby. She undid the shoulder harness, leaned over, and planted a kiss on his cheek. "Thank you for putting up with me. I'm not myself these days."

Derek pulled her under his arm. "Everything will work out, you'll see."

"This is your idea of everything working out?" Sam asked as she looked at the circus of activity around the blazing abortion clinic. Policemen and firefighters worked side-by-side, tenement neighbors clutched precious possessions, curious bystanders jockeyed for better position, and motorists rubbernecked.

Derek pulled to the curb, out of the way of the fire hoses, television cables, the bomb squad, and emergency vehicles. "Wait here," he said as he got out. She followed him across the street.

He ducked around a sentry decked out in a Los Angeles Police Department uniform and rushed up to the fireman holding a bullhorn. Sam could have heard what they were shouting to each other better if the sentry wasn't holding her back and screaming in her ear that the area was off limits. How stupid did he think she was? Her plea that she worked there fell on deaf ears.

Not everyone was deaf. A woman leashed to a microphone and cameraman circumnavigated an oil-slick puddle to reach Sam. "You work at the Eastside Clinic, I understand," the woman said a nanosecond before shoving the mike under Sam's nose.

Sam, caught in a lie, was speechless. She couldn't focus on what to say; in fact, she couldn't get her thoughts off the woman's face. Her considerable makeup was flawless. She had to have lost a good hour's sleep applying it. Sam couldn't remember the last time she had had even a breath of makeup on her face.

"Is this bombing the work of right-to-lifers?" the woman got in just as Sam answered her first question.

"No, the truth is—"

Derek pulled her away and hustled her back across the street only steps ahead of the newswoman and her cameraman. "Weren't you supposed to stay in the car?"

Who was he to give her orders? She beat him to the door handle, opened it herself, and jerked her arm away when he tried to help her into the car. They slammed the door together.

He jumped behind the steering wheel and took off like a bat out of hell. "No one was inside," Derek told her when they were well away from the frenzied scene.

"What are we going to do now?" Sam asked.

"Pay the good doctor a house call."

Alan Martin's apartment door was ajar. It wasn't a good sign. Sam waited for Derek to decide. He pressed the doorbell. There was no answer.

Besides learning Dr. Martin's address, Derek had also discovered that he didn't have a wife and child to take to the zoo.

"The door *is* open." Sam didn't altogether like the look Derek gave her. "What if he's ill and not able to summon help? I'm a doctor, I really should go in and make sure."

"Wait here." Derek pushed the door open and stuck his head in. "Dr. Martin, are you home?" He stepped in.

Sam looked around the swimming pool area in the middle of the apartment building complex and then around the apartments. No one was in sight, though that didn't mean they weren't peeking out from behind curtains. Sam followed Derek in.

They were not Martin's first visitors, if Sam could go by the looks of the front room. Sam thought she recognized the handiwork of the same person or persons who had trashed the Smiths' hotel room.

"Where are you, Derek?"

"In the bathroom, don't come in."

She found him in the bathroom, staring up at Alan Martin. "How stupid could he be!" Martin was strung up over the sagging shower-curtain rod to look like a case of autoerotic asphyxia, wearing nothing but twin binding around his wrists. "He could have done something unique."

"I'd call this pretty unique, Samantha. But I don't think he did it."

"Martin? No, I meant the killer, or killers." She laughed at the irony. "At least he was paying a little attention to Dr. Sommers' presentation."

Derek looked at her questioningly.

"Dr. Sommers showed a slide of an autoerotic asphyxia case minutes before Doyle was killed." Sam looked first at his dangling feet. She may have stepped up to the plate prematurely. She noted the considerable postural swelling of the ankles, a result of hanging for several hours. But of more interest were the Tardieu's spots, petechial hemorrhages, named after the French medicologist who first described them. These pinhead-sized hemorrhages in the skin indicated leakage of blood through capillaries owing to over-congestion, and occurred most often in cases where the mechanism of death was asphyxial.

She handed Derek her purse so she could climb up on the seat of the toilet to get a better look at the noose around his neck. "He should have put a towel under the rope. That is, if he wanted people to think this was an accident."

"What are you doing?" Derek tried to lift her down, but she slapped his hand away.

"I'm looking at the corpse. Something tells me this is going to be my last look at Alan Martin. Unless you and your superspy group can convince the LAPD to let me post him." Sam worked one leg onto the ledge of the tub to get a little leverage. Somewhere along the line she felt Derek holding her bottom. She got her hand around Alan's forearm and squeezed for all she was worth but, unlike Smith's body, no blood appeared.

"What *are* you doing?"

"Looking for the needle mark. Could you do that on the other side? I can't reach."

First he helped her down. There wasn't a trace of blood on the other arm.

"If I could only tell how he died," she said after the disappointment.

"Asphyxiation comes to mind."

The Tardieu's spots screamed out the same message, but an accidental death during an act of sex perversion was just too hard to swallow. The death tableau was straight out of Dr. Sommers's slide show. "So where's the wife and kid he took to the zoo? What's the odds of his abortion clinic being bombed on the same night he accidentally kills himself?"

Derek sighed. "You're right." He sniffed, closed in on the corpse, and took in a deep breath. He looked like Lewis Carroll's Cheshire cat when he exhaled. "Do you smell almonds?"

She didn't, but that was okay. The bittersweet smell of almonds indicated the presence of cyanide, a class-six supertoxin, which only one in five people could detect. Apparently Derek was that one in five, if not one in a million.

Sam loved it. "Cyanide's perfect. It prevents the cells from utilizing the available oxygen in the body. The oxygen-starved cells shut down, brain functions cease, the lungs

suspend breathing. Mirroring asphyxiation." And explaining the petechial hemorrhagic spots. "Then, assuming the
medical examiner didn't detect the telltale odor and released
the body, the embalming fluid would break down the
cyanide, destroying all evidence of foul play."

Derek took her hand. "Then let's go."

"Go? Aren't we going to call the police?"

"No. We're going to sit back and see who discovers and
then who claims the body."

15

"ARE YOU ALL right, Samantha?"

Would this solicitous behavior of Derek's never end? No, she wasn't all right. She was sicker than a dog. It was hotter than hell in the back of the empty courtroom, the baby was kicking up a storm, and her pyloric sphincter threatened to erupt like Mount Vesuvius. How much longer did they have to wait for the judge to return from his chambers?

Derek tried to hold her hand; instead she placed his over the thumping. His eyes danced with surprise, and suddenly it didn't matter how bad she felt.

"You the Hermans?" asked the bony officer, who had slipped in behind them with his short, pudgy sidekick.

Derek withdrew his hand as he turned around and got to his feet. "Turners."

The taller official looked at his clipboard. "Turner? Isn't the next case—"

"We're the quick wedding between the divorces."

"Well put, my darling." She stretched to her full height, leaving nothing to their imaginations. And why not? She was never going to see these two again. And what did she care, anyway? Wasn't she Sheridan's prime source of gossip these days?

"Well," the pudgy officer patted the gun on his hip, "we'll stick around—make sure he says 'I do.' "

"You mean make sure *she* says 'I do,' " Derek insisted.

The guys were real charmers. The taller, older one found

his wallet and flipped out the credit-card holder like a runaway accordion to display years of school pictures. The younger showed a lonely baby picture his wife had taken at J. C. Penney.

Memories of her marriage to John flooded back to her. She had nixed Derek's suggestion to have June and Chris stand up with them because they had at her wedding to John. She just wanted this over and done with so that they could get on with their lives. *Something old, something new, something borrowed, something blue.* She was old, the baby was new, the guys were loaning her their guns, and her pale pink smock was cross-stitched in blue. "The ring!"

"Right here." He patted his breast pocket.

"No, *your* ring."

"Would I give you an excuse?" He patted his pocket again.

She shifted uncomfortably and pushed against her bulging side, trying to move the little appendage that was kicking her rib.

It didn't get by supersleuth. He slipped his hand under hers. "What is this?"

"A tiny foot."

He beamed from ear to ear. It was the one memory of their wedding day she hoped to hold.

"We're going to be fashionably late at the very least, Aunt June. . . . She's stretched out on the bed right now, but I suspect she'll be holding court in the throne room in a minute. . . . Except she can't remember which cheek goes on it."

Was it too much to ask of life not to be the butt of everyone's jokes? Sam groaned and buried her face in the pillow, smelling the faintest trace of Derek's aftershave.

"At the Grille . . . we'll be there."

She groaned louder after he hung up. "Couldn't you've begged off?"

He outlined her butterfly. "We won't stay for dessert. Have to get back for the eleven o'clock news." He pushed her hair away from her forehead. They were both looking at the beads of sweat on his fingertips. "Are you sure you're not coming down with something?"

"I wish I were. It's been the same pattern for months."

Derek stroked her hair. "Maybe you should eat more frequently."

She could barely find time for three meals. "Thought I was the doctor."

"Doctors make the worst patients." He brushed lazy lips across her cheek. "By the way, before he left, Sommers gave Chris a copy of the autopsy report to give to you." Gentle hands massaged her tired back. How did he always know the right spot?

"What did it say?"

"Lethal injection, but not cyanide. You'll see it soon enough. Something to drink? Seven-Up, Alka-Seltzer?"

"Alka-Seltzer!" Sam scrambled up and ran to the bathroom.

Derek followed. She vaguely felt him gather up her hair. It was comforting to know someone loved her enough to support her head while she was being so disgusting.

"No dessert?" Chris asked as he inspected the pastry tray.

"None for me," Derek said.

Sam looked at her watch. The spy-type Derek had called about Alan Martin told him to catch Channel Ten at eleven.

Chris waved the pastry tray away.

"*You're* not having dessert?" Sam asked in true amazement. She expected her remark to slide right over the top of his glistening head.

June swallowed a grin.

Chris nodded to the waiter.

Sam smelled a rat.

The notion of a quick farewell-we'll-see-you-in-another-seven-years flew out the window as the waiter returned with a small cake topped by bride and groom figurines.

"Chris, you old sentimental fool!" Sam exclaimed as the

cake was placed in front of her. "Everyone's staring," she whispered across the table.

With the flare of a practiced host, Chris poured champagne all around. "A toast." He waited until all had picked up their goblets. "To Mr. and Mrs. Turner, may your marriage be as happy as . . . June's."

"If not happier," June added.

"Hear, hear," Derek said above the clanging goblets.

Sam sipped as the others drained their glasses. After slices of cake were passed, Sam asked, "Did you read the report, Chris?" She was still ticked that he wouldn't tell her what Sommers had said about the autopsy.

"I glanced at it. June forgot to remind me to bring it down. I'll bring it to your room after dinner."

"An antiarrhythmic drug, right?"

"All that can wait, Sam. We're celebrating a very important event. A milestone in our lives." Chris refilled the goblets. "And to John. I know how happy this marriage would have made him." June kicked him under the table. Sam knew because she'd caught a piece of it. "Maybe I didn't say that right. I mean now that he's dead."

"I'm sure Dad would be relieved to know that his son is caring for the woman he so deeply loved and at the same time that woman was making his son the happiest man alive."

"I'll drink to that," June said.

"Yes, yes, that's what I meant."

Sam silently put the goblet to her lips. Today of all days she didn't want to be reminded of John. Her guilt at remarrying was still high. "Which one, Chris?"

"What?" he asked, a forkful of white cake to his mouth.

"Which antiarrhythmic?"

"Bretylium."

Sam sighed. "Too bad it wasn't something exotic we could trace. Cyanide isn't going to help either." Few suppliers kept detailed records of purchasers.

"What cyanide?" Chris asked.

"We suspect Alan Martin died of cyanide poisoning," Sam explained.

"He's dead?"

"As dead as any corpse that's graced your table."

"Sodium cyanide or potassium cyanide?" Chris asked out of idle academic curiosity.

Sam shrugged.

"IM, IV, or ingested?"

Sam shrugged again. "Speculation, Chris, that's all it is. Derek's the one who detected the almond odor. I couldn't smell it."

Chris sighed and propped his head in his hands. "I never could either, but John had the gift."

$\triangledown$

16

DEREK FLIPPED TO Channel Ten and then crawled over the bed where Sam was propped up, the autopsy report in her lap. "I should get you a job doing that," he said, thumbing at the television doctor holding up an over-the-counter cure for the most insidious yeast infections.

Sam moaned something about being asleep. Derek's wedding night was not shaping up to be as memorable as his high-school health teacher had led him to believe it would be.

The bombing of an abortion clinic did not rate lead position on the nightly news. By the time Derek was up on the latest in soap, toilet paper, and jeans, and Sam was well on the way to lullaby-land, the anchorwoman finally announced the bombing and showed a montage of the morning's frenzy. "We go now to Barbara Lopez with this exclusive interview taped earlier."

After a tawdry three-second delayed dissolve their Barbara Lopez and his Samantha filled the screen.

"Samantha, I think you're going to want to see this."

"Is this bombing the work of right-to-lifers?" Barbara asked Samantha.

"No, the truth is—"

The cameraman had managed a quick profile of Derek, and then a long shot of him dragging Samantha across the street. "Anyone knowing the whereabouts of this witness is asked to contact the LAPD at the number at the bottom of the screen," advised the voice-over as their rented Cadillac sped away.

Derek cringed at the word "witness." Two doctors were dead; killing a witness was not altogether unreasonable. Samantha had a reservation out on the morning flight. Securing a seat on the flight for himself was one of the many arrangements he would see to after she was fast asleep.

Samantha sat up and pointed to the nineteen-inch screen on the dresser. "But that's not what I meant. She asked me if I worked there. That's what I was answering." Samantha was wide awake now. She sprang out of bed and paced the floor like a caged tigress. "You didn't give me a chance to even finish my sentence." She gave the sleeves of her tight-fitting nightshirt an angry push above her elbows. Her shirttail rode up over a buttock.

Watching her rant and rave was most enjoyable.

Derek reached out and pulled her to the bed. He put a finger to her lips. "And to think, if you'd stayed in the car . . ." He lavished her with kisses. She put up a mild protest before succumbing to a higher level of communication.

Later, while watching her apply lotion to her stretched abdomen, Derek had a flutter of thought. "Samantha?"

"Hmm?"

"Do you think Tiffany might be a natural redhead?"

Her eyes were slits. The Widow Smith was not one of her favorite topics.

"Don't take it wrong. I was noticing . . . ah, you're a natural blonde and—I mean—" Derek wasn't winning his case—"maybe she and Alan Martin were siblings."

Now her eyes sparkled. "He would lie for her, kill for her."

That was a quantum leap. As great a wedding present as pinning the murder on the widow would be for Samantha, Derek simply couldn't buy it. Not in light of Martin's death. "Then why kill him? It would have taken some doing to string up his body like that."

She flopped her head down on the pillow. "Besides, the killer got the autoerotic asphyxia idea from Dr. Sommers's presentation. She wasn't there. I would have remembered *her*."

"I was thinking more along the lines of Martin being killed

because he possessed the same information as Smith."

"Then why wasn't Martin attending him? Why was Smith whispering in my ear instead of Martin's?"

She had a point. He sighed. The latest report had Tiffany Smith in Denver dealing with funeral arrangements. Nothing out of the ordinary there. And Martin's next-door neighbor discovered his body. Nothing unusual there, either. "We'll know soon enough . . . as soon as someone steps forward to claim the body." He got up and looked for his trousers. He'd hurled them a good distance. "How many people were in the room?"

Samantha shrugged. "Hundred, two hundred, three hundred for all I know."

"Did anything unusual happen?"

"I answered one of the questions . . . Chris fell asleep and started snoring, he wanted to take a walk on the—wait a minute. Two men left. They were in Doyle's general location."

"When was that?" He gave his wrinkled shirt a hardy shake.

"Just after . . . no, just before I answered the question. The commotion over Doyle was not long after that."

"What did the men look like?"

She shook her head in frustration. "I don't remember. The room was dark. When they opened the door they were shadows against bright light."

"Were they the same height?" He took the lotion and set it on the nightstand.

"Within a couple of inches, I guess."

"Tall, short, thin, fat?"

"I don't know. Average, I'd say."

He straightened the covers and tucked them around her. "Get some sleep, we have to get up early in the morning to catch our plane."

"You're going with me? What about Alan Martin's corpse and finding the murderer?"

He didn't care about solving the murders; his concern was

for Samantha's safety. "What good's a honeymoon without a bride? I'll arrange for someone to keep an eye on Martin's corpse." Derek found his cigarettes and opened the sliding door, letting in the sea breeze.

He looked beyond the glowing tip of his cigarette into the darkness. What morbid fascination drew Samantha to murder? Why did she have to right the world's wrongs? Why couldn't she wear blinders like everyone else? And why did she have to make him feel guilty about smoking?

$\triangledown$

17

"STAND HERE AND guard these pigs while I chase down some change." Derek left Samantha loitering in front of a bank of lockers while he zigzagged through the crowded airport to the newsstand. The descent into Denver had been choppy and, although she pretended otherwise, Samantha was sick again.

Derek had planned to use the three hours between flights to visit Doyle's widow. Martin's California medical license proved very interesting. He was a Harvard Medical School graduate; class of sixty-two. The Dr. Martin hanging in the bathroom couldn't possibly have been that old.

After standing in the slow line at the buzzing concessioner's dream location waiting for change in order to rid himself of the ceramic piggy banks, Derek made his way back through the crowded concourse. "All right, I have the quarters," Derek said, bending under the wide-brim hat to give Samantha a reassuring peck on the cheek. "The two little piggies will be safe and sound, now."

"I hope Lindsey and Amy appreciate them; they've been quite a nuisance."

The understatement of the year. Derek stowed the first one, pocketing the key. "Nuisance? Just because we checked all our other luggage in favor of these as carry-on and then the petite things didn't quite fit under our seats?"

"Well, if you hadn't insisted on going to Mexico—"

"You wouldn't have won the Exacta." He deposited the other three quarters in the next available locker and pocketed the key. Free from his burden, Derek took hers—a trench coat and the oversized satchel she termed a purse. "Now, my dear, instead of accompanying me to the Widow Smith's why don't you go to the restaurant and have a leisurely lunch? You didn't touch your breakfast."

"You expected me to eat that plane slop?" She took his arm in an act of finality. "We'll pay our respects together."

The hustle and bustle inside the terminal was nothing compared to curbside. Here Denver travelers popped in and out of idling cars standing three deep at the curb. Others, burdened by all types of luggage—though no pigs—dodged moving cars to reach the massive parking structure. The constant traffic noises, slamming of doors, and blaring of horns competed with the shrill-voiced message from hidden speakers that unattended vehicles would be towed away.

Derek put Samantha's coat around her shoulders as they worked their way slowly up the long cab line. "You all right?"

Samantha smiled reassuringly. "Fine. Now don't ask me again. Ever." The slightest scrutiny told of her utter exhaustion.

"Third and Krameria," he instructed the cabbie as he helped Samantha into the taxi.

The Smiths' sprawling brick ranch-style house was on the west side of the street. Except for a huge evergreen, the yard's trees boasted a handful of yellow leaves that, through no fault of their own, still cleaved to the naked limbs.

"Wait for us," Derek told the cab driver.

They crushed the brittle leaves underfoot as they made their way up the driveway, blocked by a dark blue Riviera bearing Arizona license plates.

"Looks like the family's gathering round," he said as he plucked a shriveled leaf from her hat.

"Tomorrow's the funeral, isn't that what *Tiffany* told you?" she asked breathlessly.

He was becoming accustomed to the way Samantha made Mrs. Smith's name sound like a four-letter word. "Ten o'clock tomorrow morning."

For a split second Tiffany seemed surprised to see them. Odd, since he had called to say they were on their way. "Derek, Dr. Turner, thank you for coming." Sweetness dripped from the words. "Come in." She led them through the hallway into the living room. An elderly, stooped man rose from one of the two pastel chairs; the woman—presumably the owner of the walker next to the yellow print couch—remained seated. "Mom and Dad, these are the Turners I told you about. Derek, Dr. Turner, my hus . . . band's parents." She took the shredded tissue and dabbed her eyes. It was a good try.

Samantha moved, with more alacrity than Derek would have thought possible, to the old man and shook his hand. Once he had been tall, now his bones had settled into an S curve. His scant hair was white and stood straight up like a punker's. "I'm so sorry we meet under these circumstances," Samantha told the grieving old man. Derek could think of nothing in life more painful than burying one's child.

"Thank you."

He greeted Derek with a handshake. Derek's eyes followed Samantha as she took a seat beside the doctor's mother. "My daughter-in-law tells us that you were the one who tried to revive our son after his heart attack." Derek noticed a flash of anger cross Samantha's face at the words "heart attack." "Please accept our gratitude." His words were loud, typical of the hard-of-hearing.

"It was my wife who tried to help your son," Derek explained loudly. "Samantha is the doctor in the family."

Mr. Smith stared questioningly at his daughter-in-law, who had just taken the matching chair near the couch. He took a hesitant step toward his wife. "He says it was his wife who tried to help Doyle."

Mrs. Smith turned to Samantha, her gnarled hand reaching out for Samantha's wrist. "Thank you, dear." The woman's choking words were a great deal softer than her husband's.

"I'm only sorry we weren't able to save him." Less than

subtly, Samantha turned her attention to the young widow. "What are your plans now, Mrs. Smith?"

With an affected start, Tiffany lifted her eyes over the top of the tissue. "I—I really don't have any plans. Doyle was my whole—" Her words turned to jagged sobs.

Derek dutifully patted Tiffany's shoulder, ignoring Samantha's glacial stare.

"Are your parents also here to help you through this?" Samantha's voice was as smooth as glass.

"What did she say?" Mr. Smith shouted.

"She wants to know if Tiffany's parents are here, dear," the frail woman hollered back. "He's so vain he won't admit he's hard-of-hearing. Tiffany's parents are deceased. Poor dear has no one now."

Tiffany sniffed and smiled at her mother-in-law. "That's not true, Mom, I have you," her voice rose, "and Dad."

"What did she say?" Mr. Smith asked.

The young widow crossed her shapely legs. Derek followed the movement, but did not allow himself the luxury of lingering. In a second he was holding Samantha's cold gaze.

"I said I'm thankful that I have you and Mom to lean on during this stressful time."

Mr. Smith nodded.

"No brothers or sisters?" Samantha asked, her voice all innocence and concern.

Tiffany shook her head.

"I lost my first husband to a coronary. My sister's husband took charge of all the arrangements," Samantha explained, more as an apology for asking than an indictment of Derek and his two sisters. He had been in Afghanistan and hadn't learned of his father's death until several weeks after the fact; nonetheless, a pang of guilt surfaced. "My grief has lasted for more years than we were married." She turned to the younger Mrs. Smith. "How many years were you married?"

Tiffany gave Samantha her full attention, but the elder Mrs. Smith answered. "The poor dears hadn't celebrated their first anniversary. Doyle was her second husband. Her first husband was killed in a car crash. Four kids were in the other car, all seriously injured. None of them died."

"Doyle and my first husband were golf partners."

"What did she say?"

His question went unanswered as Samantha rose. "Do you mind if I use your bathroom?"

Tiffany started to speak, but Mrs. Smith was in ahead of her. She raised her arm and pointed the knotted hand toward the hall. "It's the first door on the right."

"Morning sickness still," Derek assured them loudly after she'd disappeared from view.

"I remember how sick I was when I carried Doyle." Mrs. Smith nodded painfully. "But it was all worth it. Doyle was such a happy baby, never fussy."

Derek divided his attention among the three mourners as the elder Mrs. Smith tearfully revisited her son's childhood. Mr. Smith sat patiently by, nodding at inappropriate times. The younger woman endured the ordeal with just the right amount of sentiment. Tiffany didn't seem broken up over her husband's death; whether she was responsible or an accessory remained to be seen. When Mrs. Smith paused between memories, Derek spoke. "I wonder if you'll excuse me a moment, I'd better check on my wife."

Tiffany sprang from her chair. "I'll go along and see if I can be of any help."

"The bathroom is—"

Tiffany twirled around to look at her tiresome mother-in-law. "Yes, I know where it is. This is *my* house now."

"How silly of me," Mrs. Smith said, giving a little embarrassed titter.

"They lived here before they retired to Arizona. Sometimes they forget they've moved," Tiffany explained quasicharitably in the hallway, out of Mrs. Smith's earshot, and certainly out of Mr. Smith's.

Derek knocked at the bathroom door. "Samantha, are you all right?" He turned to Tiffany, whose gorgeous wide eyes had dried nicely. A breath of mascara streaked her cheek. "Perhaps I should go in alone."

Tiffany nodded absently. "Could I get her something to drink? Would *you* like something to drink?"

"We really need to be going. She'll be all right, I'm sure." Concerned, he knocked again. "Samantha?" When Tiffany turned to leave, he cracked the door and peeked in. A sick sense overwhelmed him. Derek waited until Tiffany turned back to look before he stepped into the empty room. "Will you never learn?" he muttered to himself. Stepping back into the hall, he closed the door behind him and returned to the living room.

"Is she okay?"

Derek nodded. It seemed an eternity before he heard the toilet flush.

Samantha returned to her chair and received the elder Mrs. Smith's full commiseration and the history of the woman's pregnancy, which only Samantha and Mr. Smith had missed at the first telling.

Derek crossed to Samantha's side and helped her up. "We really must be going if we're to catch our plane and get home. I can't remember a more unpleasant vacation. Between your husband's death and Dr. Martin's death—" Derek broke off and shook his head.

Tiffany's mask fell away. She staggered back to her chair and sat down.

"Someone else died at the convention?" Doyle's mother asked.

"A young kid from LA. Tragic." Derek glanced at Tiffany. She was traumatized. The trip had been worthwhile.

They were well down the path when Samantha said, "She didn't know about Martin's death. And it bothered her more than her husband's."

"Where were you?"

"What?"

"When you weren't in the bathroom."

Samantha looked over her shoulder at the house. "In the den. Got his typewriter ribbon."

Derek broke stride for only a second. He opened the taxi's door and ushered her in. "And you replaced it with?"

Chagrined, she looked over at him. "Nothing?"

"Think she might notice?"

She looked out the window.

The ride back proved long. As soon as they stepped out of the cab—this time in front of the annex building housing the commuter airlines—Samantha said, "You know, I'd rather you'd yell at me than speak as if you were reasoning with a naughty child."

And he would rather he hadn't given her the time to let it fester. "Did I say something to offend you?"

She whirled around, a silhouette against the haze of the soft pink sunset fading fast behind the Rockies. " 'Think she might notice?' " she mimicked. She rearranged the purse strap on her shoulder, flinging her chin high in the air as she started toward the building. "So what? Was I supposed to leave it because she might notice? Didn't Doyle ask me to send the letter to the authorities? Doesn't it make sense that if I couldn't get the letter I should reconstruct it? It was his property, wasn't it? He entrusted it to me, didn't he? I'm fed up with the whole business."

Derek grabbed a flailing arm and pulled her out of the way of a electric cart.

"I was just trying to help the man," she said without skipping a beat. "The way I remember it, he was murdered and asked for my help. I'm sorry I ever got involved."

As was Derek. He opened the glass door for her, but she didn't notice. She was squinting into the slanting sun at a black Lexus. Derek caught only a glimpse of a gray arm as the passenger door closed. The tinted windows restricted further scrutiny. "What is it?"

"Do you know that man?"

"No."

She continued to stare until the car merged and disappeared into the steady stream of traffic. "He recognized us."

"Why do you say that?"

"He put his hand up to his face when he went by."

Derek would have been more concerned if they were still in LA, where Samantha had graced the Channel Ten news. Also if the man had tried something. Walking was not an indication of hostility. "He was probably trying to keep the sun out of his eyes."

She nodded. "Oh, I see. He's one of your buddies and he didn't want *me* to see him."

Derek took Samantha's arm and guided her through the door. She twisted away from him once they were inside. He wouldn't insist. He hadn't seen the man, but it was unlikely that it was anyone he knew. Not that he was going to plead his case in such an open forum. He stole a look at her pursed lips, wondering if he would ever gain her absolute trust.

She passed the check-in counter, slammed her purse onto the conveyor belt, and stomped through the metal detector. Marriage had its downside.

He watched her take a seat in a row of black plastic chairs in the large crowded waiting room.

"Don't concern yourself with checking in, I'm happy to do it for you," he mumbled to himself as he headed to the check-in counter. Traveling had certainly taken its toll and he'd be happy to get her home. He hoped he'd be out of the doghouse by then.

"Dr. Turner has a seat assignment, but I'm flying standby. Will there be a problem getting on the flight?" He hadn't had the luxury of knowing his plans until he had flown to California. After seeing her, all his previous plans were as brittle leaves in the wind, and the rest of life tumbled into place.

"Shouldn't be," she answered as she fingered the keyboard. "I'll go ahead and give you a seat assignment. Have nothing close to Dr. Turner's 9B. How does 3A sound?"

"As long as it's on the plane." Pocketing the tickets and boarding passes, Derek went through the metal detector and joined his wife. He moved her hat over one seat, sat down beside her. She was absently pushing on her side.

"This child and I are going to have words over his

behavior. He may have as much room as he likes out front, but not my rib cage."

Derek slipped his hand under hers to feel what she felt. "She's stopped." Derek barely got out the words before a faint flick tickled his palm. "Did you feel that, Samantha?"

She smiled, and then looked lovingly at him. "I'm sorry I snapped at you, Derek."

Derek stroked her cheek with the hand not waiting for another indication of life. He quickly folded his hands over his chest when he realized the woman across from them was staring. "How about a little something from the vending machine to tide you over?"

"I am beginning to feel that all-too-familiar queasiness again. Maybe something salty. Some potato chips or . . . the pigs!"

The damn pigs! Derek looked at his watch. Fifteen minutes before the flight and the pigs were in the other terminal building—the one connected by a shuttle system. He had half a mind to leave them where they were, but something told him it was a minority opinion. "I'll go for them." He rose. "If I don't get back in time I'll take the morning flight, but don't you miss the plane waiting for me," Derek added as he separated the tickets and handed over hers along with one of the boarding passes. "I love you," he added, kissing her forehead.

"I would stay here with you, but I really do have to be at work in the morning," she shouted as he backed away.

"Be right back."

Derek turned the corner and raced down the corridor. A long line of travelers from the Aspen flight, which had just landed twenty minutes behind schedule, received him. "Excuse me, excuse me," he said as he pushed through the deep line, "have a plane to catch in fifteen minutes."

"Lucky you. Mine's in ten."

He stopped a moment and looked at the tiny middle-aged woman, and then over the heads to the door. "Give me your makeup case. Let's see if we can make the shuttle."

Derek pushed to the head of the line, the woman behind him. A few well-chosen words to the uniformed attendant brought the full shuttle to a halt. Derek and the woman hurried aboard. Standing in the aisle gave them the advantage of being the first two off. Derek carried the woman's case up the outdoor staircase, wishing he hadn't offered to help. Racing up the steps two at a time would have saved precious time. Once they were inside, he handed the woman the case and was gone.

The trip back, saddled with two pigs, was much more frustrating. Derek had glanced at his watch no fewer than ten times in the last minute. He was waiting, impatiently, for the bus to unload the infinitely slow passengers, each having to retrieve at least one piece of luggage from the rack behind the driver. At last the attendant unsnapped the cable rope for Derek and three other travelers.

"Any possibility of getting there pronto?"

"You again? Weren't you just—"

Derek held the pigs out. "I'm on the Sheridan flight."

After his fellow travelers had in turn placed cumbersome bundles on the rack, the driver logged the time on her clipboard, radioed for clearance, and started the tortoise trip to the annex terminal. "We've got one for the Sheridan flight," she reported over her radio.

"Will let them know," came the static reply.

She called over her shoulder as she waited for a baggage train to move out of the way. "They'll wait for you."

Why didn't he believe her?

When the bus lurched in front of the small building, Derek was off like a shot, running through the corridor into the waiting area, pushing through bustling crowds to the departure door. "I'm on the Sheridan flight. Has it left?"

The hassled ticket taker nodded and pushed his spectacles up with the back of his hand. "This is the flight to Cody."

"The shuttle driver said you're holding the plane for me."

"I don't know why they always say that." The man

pointed toward the desk at the other side of the room. "Check with them."

Derek ran to the desk. "Has the flight to Sheridan left?"

A practiced smile came to the receptionist's lips much faster than she came to the counter. "Sheridan, you say?"

Derek put down the menacing pigs and took out his ticket. "Flight three nine two six."

She punched the code into her computer. "Left at five-twenty-five." She smiled sympathetically. "Sorry."

Derek looked at his watch. Five minutes! He couldn't remember the last flight he'd been on that had pulled away on time. Derek looked out the window to be certain and then around the room to make sure Samantha hadn't waited for him. He sighed disgustedly and then turned back to the woman. "Need to reserve a seat on the morning flight."

The woman nodded knowingly. Her time-worn creases deepened as she stared at the computer. "It's full." She looked up at him. "I could wait-list you?"

"How can I get to Sheridan tonight?"

She nodded to the knot of passengers at the other side of the room. "Cody. It's boarding now. You could rent a car from there."

Cody was a far cry from being close to Sheridan. It was way on the other side of the mountain in the northwest corner of the state. "Nothing else? One of the other carriers, maybe?" He gave her his best smile.

She leaned over the counter as if telling him something out of school. "Western has an evening flight to Casper."

Derek winked his thanks. Picking up the two pigs, which were about to be placed on the endangered species list, he headed for the shuttle bus.

▽

18

Sam, LAST IN line, watched for Derek all the way to the boarding gate. Now he'd never forgive her for buying those pigs. As she straggled behind the other passengers down the long corridor to the plane, she felt the too-familiar acid taste erupt in her throat. She ran back to the terminal to the ladies' room.

She emerged to hear the last call for the Cody flight. The thought flashed through her mind to get on that flight. Emil could come for her. Sheridan was five hours from Cody. The plane took two. She could drive from Denver to Sheridan in eight, possibly seven.

Sam looked around the room. If Derek had made it back in time, he would have gotten off as soon as he noticed she wasn't on the plane. Otherwise he was still here somewhere. After a few minutes of searching and a package of peanut butter and crackers, she headed toward the crowded gate counter. "I missed my plane to Sheridan," she told the young man with the ill-fitting glasses, "but I wonder if you can tell me if my husband made it. Or if you could page him for me or something."

He started to point toward the reservation desk, but then he changed his mind. Sam thought it had something to do with the tiny pink, blue, yellow, and aqua ducks on her maternity smock at which he was staring. She had half a notion to tell him it was borrowed. "What's the name?"

"Derek Turner." Sam looked over his shoulder as he worked on the computer.

"Three A," he muttered as he picked up the boarding passes. He shuffled through them until he picked out 3A. "Here it is. He's on the flight."

Why hadn't he gotten off? "Must have gotten on at the last moment." Wasn't he in for a surprise! She smiled at him. "Thanks."

Sam picked up a sandwich at an Arby's drive-through window and was halfway out of Denver before she discovered that the cruise control of the big blue Oldsmobile didn't work. She thought about taking it back to the airport but decided it was not worth the hour it would cost. She would simply complain to herself, or to the baby, now that he was awake and stirring inside her. "One of us should get some sleep, and since I'm the one doing the driving, I suggest it be you." Sam put the palm of her hand to the space just under her rib and pushed down. "Find another cubbyhole." The sprawling lights of civilization along the hundred miles of highway before the Wyoming border gave way to the harvest moon after Cheyenne. She settled back in a semi-comfortable position and pressed her foot a little harder on the pedal.

▽

19

Dᴇʀᴇᴋ ꜱᴛᴇᴘᴘᴇᴅ ᴏꜰꜰ the plane in Casper with a piggy bank attached to each hand and a diaper bag over his shoulder. He waited silently as Debbie's parents made a fuss over the towhead toddler half-hidden behind Debbie's legs. When Grandma had captured the screaming and kicking boy, Debbie explained to her father that she had promised her fellow traveler a ride to Kaycee.

The father looked him over. "You have folks there?"

"Live outside of Big Horn. Missed the Sheridan plane. Thought I'd call the hired hand and ask him to meet me in Kaycee, if you don't mind giving me a lift."

"Frank Collins," the man said, offering his hand.

"Derek Turner."

"Turner? The buffalo ranch?"

"My wife's."

He lifted a brow. "Know the feeling."

Derek let it go. While everyone else was claiming baggage, he tried the ranch number. Emil didn't answer. Samantha's plane would be landing in a while. He could call the airport in Sheridan and leave a message for her to send Emil to Kaycee but, knowing Samantha, she'd show up instead. The last thing he wanted was having her out on the highway alone. He and the pigs would hitch from Kaycee.

Debbie and rambunctious Randy had come from Atlanta, where Randy's father had seen them off early that morning before he started a year's tour of duty in Greenland. Their furniture and cooking utensils would be stored, but many of their things would be needed during their year's stay in Kaycee. Derek began to wonder if there would be room for him in the car after he saw all of the boxes around Frank's feet.

▽

20

Aᴛᴇʀ ꜰɪᴅᴅʟɪɴɢ ᴡɪᴛʜ the radio, trying to recapture the Oklahoma talk show, Sam turned it off. She cursed the rented car. Was it too much to ask to have a little company on the deserted road? In the last hour she had passed two moving objects, an eighteen-wheeler and a station wagon. A fox, two skunks, and three deer adorned the shoulder of the road. She knew other animals roamed over the miles and miles of prairie, but now that the moon was down she couldn't see them.

The dash light wasn't working so she couldn't tell the time. She had passed Glendo and was on the long stretch to Douglas, which would mark the halfway point. Sam was beginning to doubt the success of this folly. She was tired, irritable, and uncomfortable. Her dexterity was shot and her eyes were heavy. She was improvising a scenario where she'd spend the night in Douglas, get on the road by four, and still be at work by eight. Perhaps she could call Eugene and ask him to postpone his trip to Salt Lake for a day. He'd love that. Maybe he would, it was his wife's family reunion. She wouldn't ask. If only her eyes weren't so heavy.

▽

21

DEREK WAS IN LUCK. A highway patrol car was idling in front of Kaycee's Texaco station. He stumbled over a box getting out of the Suburban, but the damn pigs were just fine. "Thanks for the ride."

"You sure your folks are going to meet you?" Frank asked.

"Should be here soon. Thanks again." He waited until they were well away before heading inside. The highway patrol officer divided his attention between the young woman filling his styrofoam cup with coffee and Derek. A man carrying two overgrown piggy banks into a service station was no doubt suspect. Should he say, "This is a stickup. Put all your change into the banks?" He said hello instead.

"Car trouble?" the officer asked.

Derek placed the pigs beside the door. "Plane trouble." He didn't miss the anxious glance the two exchanged. "Missed the plane to Sheridan."

The woman tried to pour more coffee into the patrolman's cup. It ran over the officer's arm. He didn't notice at first. It hit Derek square in the bowels of his being. The officer spoke. "You were supposed to be on that Sheridan flight?"

Derek's hand started shaking before his mind could formulate the reason for his question. "What about the plane?"

The trooper found napkins and wiped his arm. "Crashed as it was about to land. I'm on my way up there now."

It was as if someone jammed a fist down his throat and ripped out his insides. Derek had a momentary loss of equilibrium, then found his tongue to ask, "Were there survivors?"

"Don't see how there could have been . . . augured into the field just shy of the highway." He pulled one napkin after the other out of the dispenser until the woman moved it away. "You're one lucky man."

Derek stared at the man, his whole body numb. "My wife was on that plane."

$\triangledown$

22

Sam's back was killing her. And the baby kicked for all he was worth. How could such a little thing cause her so much discomfort? The only good thing now was the blur of light ahead. Sheridan.

The dense fog masked the terrain, and Sam lost all perception of distance. She assumed she was close to the Big Horn turnoff if the creepy glow of light was any indication. She crept along hoping she would be able to see the exit.

She sensed, more than saw, someone looming ahead of her in the middle of the highway. A man waving her to the left: the sheriff. She was never so glad to see him. She rolled down the window and stopped beside him.

"Is that you, Doc Turner?"

"An accident, Hank? Do you need my help?"

"They said you were on the plane."

"No, missed the plane. Had to drive. Can't see a damned thing; how far to the turnoff?"

"Half mile at most."

"So. Anyone injured? Need my help?" she asked again to prod him.

"Beyond needing help," he answered, looking behind her car into the fog. "It can wait until morning."

Welcome back to work! Sam heard a blend of voices shouting behind the curtain of heavy mist. She suspected the fire department, ambulance, highway patrol, and wrecker were all present. As coroner, she'd look the scene over and maybe save herself a trip in the morning. Big difference seeing the scene during the day, but if it were routine, it wouldn't matter all that much. "Might as well look as long as I'm here. Should I park here?"

"Pull up about fifty yards where the fence is cut. It starts about a hundred yards in."

"A hundred yards? What was it? A runaway eighteen-wheeler or something?" She'd seen that smile on his face before. Embarrassment. It suddenly evoked an unendurable anguish. "What did you mean, you thought I was on the plane?"

"I, ah, I, ah," he stammered.

"The plane crashed?" Yes, she could see it on his face. It slashed through her like a red-hot knife. Derek's plane. She stomped on the accelerator and sped blindly fifty yards or so. She parked behind the fire truck and ran east, following the path of eerie red lights they'd put out. She was oblivious to the cold, to the burrs and hot embers ripping and burning holes in her nylons, to the voices that called to her telling her to stop. She needed to find Derek's body. She needed to see.

She threaded through the burnt field by instinct and was almost on top of the wreckage before she saw it and the blackened wisps of smoke losing themselves in darkness. The plane had screwed itself into the ground. The bodies would be charred and mangled. Her heart sank as she remembered Hank's words about being beyond help. Beyond hope.

It would be weeks before she would have them all identified. She remembered her fellow passengers, laughing and joking as they waited in line. A few faces had been familiar, but she'd have to have a look at the passenger list before she could match them to names. Except Derek.

She figured it was about three. It would be a good four hours before light started creeping into the eastern sky. Hopefully the sun would burn off the fog. Perhaps then she could see. She tried to clear her eyes with the back of her hand, but it didn't help. Why would she want to see the two little boys that had been racing around the chairs in the Denver airport? Their matching red corduroy jumpers would be burnt to crisps and melted into burnt flesh and bone. She didn't want to see their father, who had swooshed up the tiny one when he tripped over the ski boots of the sunburned Texan sitting across from her. The boots were almost as big as the boy. Sam would have to remember to ask for two small body bags.

"Sam, is that you?" The hand on her shoulder held her fast.

"Yes," she told Eric, one of the paramedics.

"Someone at the staging area said you were on the plane."

"No."

"Are you okay?"

"I have to remember to get two small body bags for Master Doe One and Master Doe Two."

"Let's head over to the staging area."

Sam barely felt him leading her. "No. I'm waiting for the sun to burn off the fog. I want to see the plane."

"Come on, it's been a long night. Let's get you home. Won't be anything to see until morning."

"I need to borrow a yellow slicker." Everyone on the mass-disaster team wears a yellow slicker. It was her rule.

"In the morning."

"What do you suppose happened?"

"An explosion, they say. A flash of light, then flames."

"I need to find someone." She broke away, turned, and ran back to the wreck. The baby was kicking her in the ribs again, but she let it be. Tonight she didn't care. She wished the sun would hurry. She needed to see.

"Samantha?"

A quiver crawled up her spine at the sound of John's voice. Samantha? John and everyone else called her Sam. Except Derek. Was her subconscious playing tricks on her? She turned slowly; her whole being shivered. A ghostly form shimmered in the fog. Sam held her breath as it came toward her.

"Oh, Samantha!" He forced her off balance. "I thought . . . I thought you were on the plane."

He held her so tight she could barely speak. "How did you survive the crash?"

Derek crushed her all the harder. "You weren't on the plane?"

Tears streamed unchecked over her cheeks. "I was in the ladies' room retching my brains out."

Derek laughed or cried, Sam couldn't tell which. "Thank God for morning sickness, especially in the evening."

"How did you get out alive?" She felt him take a deep breath as he tightened his grip all the more.

"I didn't get on. Those two wonderful pigs made me miss the plane. I flew to Casper."

"Casper." She laughed, a sob catching in her throat. "Wish I'd thought of that. I drove from Denver."

Derek held her at arm's length. "You drove all that way alone? Don't you know how dangerous that was?"

▽

23

IMPLEMENTING HER MASS-DISASTER plan was a first Sam would have gladly passed up. She pulled up her jeans. She'd fastened them together with string, for all the good it was doing. Her down vest covered her, she thought. It was the least of her concerns. Still she pulled the yellow slicker together and started snapping the clasps. Derek knelt down and finished the job.

The easterly sun was high enough now to see the entire field, which from the command post looked like a junkyard after incineration. The plane, minus the tail section, which had been blown to smithereens, looked like the smoldering burned-out trunk of a redwood. The manpower this was going to take was mind-boggling. Federal investigators would be arriving soon to sift through the wreckage. Cranes were being hauled in from Casper and Billings. Sam suspected all the teams would be assembled by high noon. Dark at the latest. None of that was her concern, only the forty-nine victims. Most of the bodies had been accounted for as they searched in the dark for survivors. Now it was time to move them out.

Derek gave her a reassuring squeeze, signaling his under-standing. He looked as tired as she felt. She, of course, looked much worse. They'd managed a couple of hours in bed, holding on to each other for dear life, but sleep eluded them both. Adrenaline kept her going.

"All right, folks, give me your attention," Hank hollered to the crowd of volunteers. "Thanks to all of you for comin' out to help. Couple of guidelines to run by you. Our most important goal is to find all fifty-one victims as quickly as possible." It was forty-nine—Derek and she were still on the passenger list—but she wouldn't correct him right now. "And do it in a manner so as not to do anything that might hinder the identification of a body."

"Like what?" someone at the back of the crowd yelled.

"Doc Turner will go over all that in a minute," Hank said as he scanned his list of points to cover. "We'll have to wait for the cranes to get bodies out of the plane, but there're plenty scattered about to keep us hopping. If you find a body, call out. Doc Turner wants to have a look before we move it. Move him or her."

Sam cleared her throat to get the sheriff's attention. "Relatives," she mouthed.

Hank scratched his head as if trying to recall what they'd talked about. Then he nodded. "How many of you might have a relative or loved one on the plane?"

Sam looked around to see a number of hands in the frigid air. She could appreciate their anxiety, but she couldn't have them helping. The last thing she wanted was to have relatives identify, maybe wrongly so, loved ones. Trying to talk them out of a body they've started bonding with and mourning over to replace with the one she had determined belonged to them would be harder to accomplish than scaling Cloud Peak. She didn't feel up to either. And she wasn't going to release any body until all were identified.

"Okay, you all go with Derek Turner here when we disburse." Derek would distribute them around as ancillary personnel—sentries to guard the cordoned-off area, traffic controllers, and the like. "Derek, come over here so they can see you." Derek stepped to Hank's side and gave a quick wave. He had been blocking the wind, Sam realized when he returned to her side again and she stopped shivering. There was more to it than that, she knew. Their brush with death made him all the more precious, but she had too much work to do to let herself dwell on anything but her duties. Besides, she'd drive herself crazy if she thought about what could have been.

"Doc Turner, you have some words?" Hank asked.

"Thanks," she said to Hank as she stepped to his side. It was like being in the shade of a palm tree. "And thank you all for coming out on this gloomy morning. My husband—she couldn't help hearing some stirring of surprise from some quarters, the mortician's to name one—"will videotape the vicinity around the body, as personal belongings and such might prove important in identifying the victim. So please do not move anything, no matter how seemingly unimportant, until Derek has filmed it."

A gust of wind lodged a flake of ash in her eye. She rubbed it with the back of her hand—the only part not sooty. "Each body will be given a number. Starting with Doe One. Not John or Jane, just Doe, as we won't be making the differential between sexes until later." Sam would be mightily surprised if sex could be determined at first glance of the charred remains. "A body part, making up less than half a body will be tagged with a letter and given its own body bag."

The cinder was irritating her eye to tears. "On the back of each tag, the finder should sign his name, so if we have a question later we can get hold of you. Put any personal items found around the body in a plastic bag and label it with the corresponding number of the body to help identify the victim. Most importantly, do not put more than one body part in a bag unless I confirm that they go together. Questions?" Please, Lord, don't let there be any. She was getting that queasy feeling and wanted to send them on their way before she was throwing up in front of an audience.

As they headed off to the four winds, she went over to the sheriff's Bronco and eased herself down on the open tailgate. Derek broke away from his group to see if he could do anything for her, but she shooed him away. Ditto Hank. She'd just as soon wallow in her misery uninterrupted.

Sam wished she had her microcassette recorder so she could dictate the family questionnaire. She'd use a police form for description. Physical anomalies, bone fractures, old X rays. Fingerprints wouldn't be helpful. Nor photographs. Dental records would. Rings, jewelry, watches. Purses, briefcases, carry-on luggage were iffy, but should be on the questionnaire.

She would renumber the bodies as she examined them and mark the caskets with both number and name. Hopefully, name. She would try to have all the bodies to their families before Christmas. Thanksgiving, if possible. No sense making them suffer any longer than necessary. The holiday season would be bad enough without their loved ones, but having uncertainty hanging over their heads was a cruelty she hoped to spare them.

Time. A monumental task that needed hours and hours of her time. And what about Doyle? How would Derek and she find time now?

She wasn't the first to vomit, she realized as she made her way to the first Doe. It was a gruesome sight. She looked at it the only way she could, with clinical detachment. As she did, the remains took on the appearance of a bronze statue. The Grim Reaper, his bony arm pointing the way of destruction. Prevailing wisdom labeled the assumed position as "the pugilistic attitude." The distorted body, crouched like a boxer ready to spring out at his opponent, was caused by the muscles contracting from the heat of the fire, not the barbaric practice of seeking glory by beating the opponent to a bloody pulp.

Derek capped the lens of the video camera and headed off to parts unknown. She was rewarded with a smile first.

"The bones are brittle," she warned. "Be careful transferring the remains." She had no sooner gotten the words out of her mouth when the cranium shattered as two men laid a body onto the plastic body bag.

"Dr. Turner," Eric called, "you're wanted at the hospital."

"I'm busy. What do they want?"

"Didn't say. Come on, I'll run you into town."

Sam wasn't certain how legal it was for Eric to race to town with the ambulance's lights going full bore, but she didn't think there were any police cars to worry about; they were all at the crash site.

Eric waited outside the emergency room in the ambulance bay. Sam pushed through the bay doors; the E.R. was quiet. Connie, the day-shift registered nurse, was at the nursing station, reading. A quick look at the clock on the wall and quicker calculations told Sam that Connie had already put in a couple of hours. "Anything happening?" Sam asked as she unfastened the yellow slicker and wiped beads of sweat from her neck.

Connie shook her head.

So what was so all-fire important that she was called away from the disaster site? Sam headed through the halls to the pathology department. Ken was haunting the door to the radiology department across the hall. "Well, look what the cat drug in." He tried to grab her.

"Don't, I'm filthy."

"I don't care." He wrapped her in his arms and whispered: "I was so worried when I heard about the plane crash."

"We drove."

He straight-armed her, showing smudges of soot all over his white lab coat. "We?"

"Derek and I were married in California."

Ken stood in stoic shock.

"Now don't be like that. We didn't want to marry, we had to."

"Think that's another one of Big Bob's axioms. Never agree when your friend insists her boyfriend is the lowest phylum of the animal kingdom, lest you turn around and find she married the animal." He twirled her around. "You've really let yourself go now that you're married."

Sam shook her head. "Ken, it's the worst mess I've ever seen in my life. We'll be cleaning up forever. But what's up here?"

"Nothing that I know about."

"Got a message to come in," she said pulling away. "Better go see about it. We'll catch up later. Tell Mary I want a new outfit from Sheridan Tent and Awning for a wedding present.

Her maternity clothes were on the plane. And this," she held out her yellow slicker, "doesn't make the appropriate fashion statement."

The receptionist, Kate, stuck her head out of the office. "Thought I heard you. Dr. Gordon's been looking for you. Has a breast biopsy. Is he ever mad he can't go to Salt Lake."

Sam hurried into the lab. Eugene was sitting in front of the microscope, a textbook on his lap.

"What's up, Eugene?"

"This frozen section's giving me trouble. The surgeons keep calling every five minutes."

"Move." Sam looked through the microscope. She didn't understand the problem. Pockets of cancer cells were dispersed throughout a dense desmoplastic stroma. "So?"

"I can't decide whether I should recommend a radical mastectomy, with removal of the attached pectoral muscles, or simply a radical mastectomy."

"It's not your place to do either. They want a report, not a consultation. They'll decide what's best for their patient."

"But—"

"Forget it, Eugene. And next time think a little before you press the panic button. Do you have any idea of what I'm facing out there? Use your head, okay?"

If her associate had anything to say, Sam didn't hear it. She was already running back to the ambulance.

$\triangledown$

24

DEREK DROVE INTO the National Guard lot. It had been three weeks since the crash, and Samantha was still identifying body parts. He parked his father's Mercedes next to the red Jeep Samantha had painted brown after Jeffrey had assured her it was the best way to keep from getting speeding tickets. Brown exterior with a red interior was really a disgusting combination. Perhaps it did keep the police away.

He walked briskly toward the occupied car on the far side of the parking lot, his mind racing to sort out a hundred details. A homemade explosive device of scant expertise planted in a checked suitcase was responsible for the crash. A preponderance of evidence, including the timing mechanism, linked the debris found in Sheridan with that at the LA abortion clinic. They were working under the assumption that Samantha was the intended victim.

Two FBI agents had been watching over her when he left two weeks ago; now the CIA was here. Scotty was in the driver's seat. Derek went around to the passenger side and got in out of the November gale. "What are you doing here? What happened to the FBI?"

"They packed it in after Samantha ran them off the road into what the locals call the borrow ditch."

Derek held out his hand. "Thanks, I owe you one."

"How'd it go in Prague?"

Post–cold war was anything but easy. Now the politicians didn't know who they wanted for bedfellows. "They won't make their move until after the holidays."

"Buys us a little time." Scotty rifled through a folder. "Here's the list of registered black Lexuses you wanted. Alan Martin is on it. The LA toxicology report. And the info on Doyle and Tiffany Smith."

A quick look. Tiffany MacCade had been married to Alan Martin. The husband killed in the car crash the elder Mrs. Smith spoke of, Derek presumed. She grew up in Chicago, but the address was now part of a parking complex. The young Alan Martin's body was claimed and cremated by a Los Angeles mortician, the remains delivered to Tiffany Smith in Denver. She was getting a good start on an Alan Martin–remains collection. It made some sense to have her brother—if he was her brother—take on her late husband's identity. Easier than going to medical school. Still, nothing made sense.

A black Lexus was indeed registered to Alan Martin. Tiffany, Martin's widow, must have had possession. But she would not have had time to see them off, pick up the gray-suited man, and be at the airport ahead of them.

He shuffled the papers. Cyanide. He'd be getting a hero's welcome.

"Surveillance report from Denver?"

Scotty looked for the report. "Only left the house once after her in-laws left. A trip to the Cherry Creek Shopping Mall for a long lunch with girlfriends. Two hefty deliveries from the local liquor store. What you might like is that Mrs. Smith makes late-night calls to a number listed for Carla Remington. As soon as the woman answers, she hangs up. Carla Remington, you'll be pleased to know, is a nurse at the Westside Family Planning Center. And the lab said to tell you the fingerprints on the matches were Alan Martin's."

"Strange. I offered him a cigarette and he turned me down."

Scotty looked at his watch. "If I hurry back to the ranch for my things, I can catch the turnaround flight."

How long had Scotty been in Sheridan? Long enough to know the plane schedule, which out here was as much a part of the day as the lumberyard's noon whistle. The plane's engines could be heard overhead as it made its way to Denver as people sat down to breakfast. It returned before lunch, left again at two, and was back after dinner dishes were dried and put away. More attention was paid to landings now that the plane crash was freshly etched in everyone's minds—despite hunting season, more seats were available.

"Been here long?"

"Let's put it this way. I fixed the dryer, know the names of all her bison, met her pet deer Alfred, was forgiven for my part in the Statue of Liberty debacle, saw two Saturday matinees, and am on a first-name basis with everyone at Taco John's. Your wife's partial to their Potato Olés."

"She ran the FBI off in record time." Derek gave him a hardy handshake. "I owe you big."

"You'd have done the same for me."

Except Scotty's wife didn't have a penchant for trouble. Derek gathered up the papers. "Give Madge and the boys my love," he said as he opened the door and climbed out.

"I'd say the same about your wife, but I think she would just as soon forget about my visit."

"She didn't run you off the road, did she?"

"No."

"Well, there you have it. She likes you." He smiled and slammed the door against the wind.

As he watched Scotty drive off, Derek thought of the million things he needed to take care of. Yesterday evening he'd made arrangements to sell his New York apartment and had separated the things he wanted shipped out right away. The rest of his belongings could wait until the addition to the house was completed. He hoped the architect was making good headway on the plans. Otherwise, they'd have to wait until spring.

Derek would wait until afternoon to speak to the Federal Aviation Administration inspector. He'd wait, too, until after hearing Samantha's side of the story before apologizing to the FBI.

There were forty-eight names listed on the passenger manifest, plus a pilot, copilot, and one stewardess, and yet Samantha had only forty-eight bodies. Two boarding passes were missing, 9B and 13C. Samantha was assigned 9B. Obviously, Derek had given her the wrong pass, 3A, his seat. Suspicion was consequently cast on the intended occupant of 13C, B. J. Forrest, who no one at the Denver airport remembered. Samantha believed that B. J. and the gray-suited man in the black Lexus were one and the same and that he had checked in a piece of luggage containing a bomb.

Samantha had been berating herself for not realizing in time what the man in the Lexus was up to. Reasoning with her about it not being her fault was akin to expecting a brick wall to melt away in sunlight. The registration report would not help. Derek tore out the page with Martin's name.

Why hadn't there been a second attempt on her life?

Derek's footsteps echoed as he made his way across the enormous room. Unlike the bits and pieces of metal that crammed the airport hanger, the forty-eight caskets seemed lost in the empty armory. He followed the sound of voices to one of the small rooms at the far side of the building. By the time he reached it, he could no longer see his breath.

Samantha had gotten noticeably larger in two weeks. Derek leaned against the doorjamb and admired the way she scribbled on the immense chart made of butcher paper that covered most of the wall. The young Dr. Gordon stared at a similar chart covering the adjacent wall. Samantha's chart listed the names and addresses from the passenger manifest. Each was classified by sex, age, height, weight, coloring, whether or not a dental file was on hand, and any other outstanding physical characteristics, most of the information coming from friends and family. Gordon's chart was labeled Doe 1 through Doe 48. Three-fourths of the columns were filled with information as to height, color of eyes and hair, fractures, incisions, dental work, and so on.

"No, it doesn't, Eugene. Look—" Samantha moved impatiently to his chart—"Doe Ten's hair roots showed large amounts of melanin." She returned to her chart and stabbed her pencil at the hair column. "Mr. Collins had blond hair."

"But he's the only one with a pin in his right ankle."

"He's the only one we know who had a pin in his right ankle. We could just as easily put a Doe Ten question mark beside Johnston, since he fits the rest and we don't have any info on him."

"Why would we do that?"

Samantha snapped the pencil in two. "We wouldn't! My point is, either the leg with the pin in it does not belong to Doe Ten, or there is another leg out there somewhere that has a pin in the ankle."

"It was in the same body bag."

"And put there while I was at the hospital looking at the fucking frozen section!"

"Well, you got your vacation. I'm the one who missed out."

Samantha ran her hand down the list of names on the wall. "These are the ones who missed out."

He hung his head, the toe of his shoe scraping the floor. "They should have taken the attached pectoral muscles. Didn't I say as much?" Derek didn't have the slightest idea what Dr. Gordon was talking about.

"Forget the breast biopsy. We have to concentrate on this." She sighed. "No," she said softly, "taking the pectoral muscles wouldn't have done any good. X rays were subsequently taken for complaint of lower back pain. Ken found rarefaction of the spinous process."

"They suspected metastatic disease already?"

Samantha nodded.

"Be an interesting postmortem, bet you."

"You want to bet something?" she asked with regained energy. "I'll tell you what, you take a close look at the leg. I bet a hundred dollars the tissue tears won't match."

"Too rich for my blood." Dr. Gordon ran his hand over his high forehead. "Guess I could have Daisy trace the serial number on the pin."

Samantha slammed her hand against the wall in frustration. "Yeah, Eugene, why don't you do just that." The sarcasm was thick in her voice. "Then we can send the leg on to Mr. Collins's family, not that we know which body to send."

"So what do you want me to do, Sam?"

"Jesus, Eugene, you are so slow—I want you to find the body that matches the goddamn leg."

Derek decided it was time to rescue Gordon and save his wife from apoplexy. "Samantha?"

She whirled around. "Derek! You're back."

He watched as she absently pressed against her right side. The baby must have been pushing against her rib again. "I've come to take you to lunch."

"I'm not—"

"Hungry? You never are these days, but you'll eat anyway."

"Is that—"

"An order?" Derek finished for her in a calm voice. He couldn't help noticing her slit eyes had turned in his direction. "It's whatever you want it to be."

Samantha stared at him for a very long, uncomfortable moment. She turned to the other doctor, who looked more like a short, skinny schoolboy. "Eugene, I don't believe you've had the pleasure of meeting my husband, Derek. Derek, Eugene."

"Actually, we have met." The kid's face turned beet-red as he crossed the room and offered his hand. "Glad to see you again, sir." Even the scalp under the thinning blond hair showed red.

Samantha pushed harder on her side. "Oh, yes, I guess you did at that. When I was dead."

Derek shook the cold hand as he stared at Samantha. "I'm glad you've stayed on. Samantha was working much too hard—she needed a partner."

"Well, actually, I'm not her partner. Officially I'm her employee. I haven't decided yet whether, at the end of the first year, I'll be her partner or if I'll merely share the workload and have my own office. Sam doesn't want to let Daisy go, but I think my wife should do the billing. You never know about employees."

During his speech Samantha had picked up her coat and purse and was at Derek's side. "I'll be back in a bit, Eugene. If you leave, lock up."

Derek took the coat from her.

"We finally ran the army guys out," Samantha said as she gave him a kiss. "They're next door at the college."

"I'll go with you," Eugene said. "That way we'll get back at the same time."

Samantha's arm shot through the sleeve of the fleece-lined trench coat like a bullet. "That'll be just great, Eugene!"

Derek would have to wait to hear her side of the FBI escapade.

"Wow! This is some car," Gordon said as they stood shivering in the wind. "It only has two seats. How will we all fit in?"

Instead of opening the passenger door of the Mercedes for Samantha, Derek turned and opened the left back door of the Jeep. "We'll take Samantha's car."

"Thank you," Samantha said as she got in, her voice at least as cold as the air.

Derek bent over and planted a kiss on her cheek, getting a mouthful of hair in the bargain. "It's nice to see you. Now where to?" he asked, getting behind the wheel.

"Arby's is fine," Gordon said. "It's the nearest except for the Holiday Inn, which would take too long."

"Samantha?"

"It doesn't matter to me." Food was pretty much the only thing about which she didn't have strong opinions.

"I don't usually recommend fast food, but Arby's fries are cholesterol-free. You should see some of the vessels I've seen. Clogged solid with fat. A wonder there aren't more coronaries."

"Sure you wouldn't rather eat at the Holiday Inn's salad bar?" Derek asked.

"I just told you it takes too long." Gordon waited a beat. "How much did the sports car set you back?"

Samantha tapped him on the shoulder. "It's none of your fucking business, Eugene."

Derek bundled Samantha into the building as Dr. Gordon kept up a one-sided conversation over the roaring wind. Something about the *Consumer Reports* article he'd read on the safety of Mercedes automobiles.

"What's your pleasure, babe?" Derek asked as they stood in line.

"A Junior, some cholesterol-free curly fries, and water to wash down the grease. I'm going to the rest room."

Derek stopped her. "Why?"

"To wash my hands. Is that all right?" she asked, dryly.

He pulled her close. "Sorry, thought maybe you were sick. I was going to offer to hold your head."

"No, I'm over all that." She smiled up at him. "But it was sweet of you to offer. I'll be right back."

With tray in hand, Derek started for an empty booth against the bank of windows, but turned down the middle aisle when he spotted the radiologist's wife. "Mary, I haven't seen you since—" Derek left the rest unsaid. He'd just as soon forget about Samantha's "funeral." He turned to the little girl across from her, her name escaping him. "My, you've grown!"

"Lindsey's in kindergarten now." Yes, Lindsey. How could he forget? The pigs were for Lindsey and Amy. Amy being Bob's daughter. "Just picked her up. Thought we girls would do lunch before picking up the baby. Join us."

"Well—"

"Oh," her voice fell, "you've got Flash with you."

"Flash?"

"Flash Gordon." Mary patted the seat beside her. "Sit."

"Samantha's coming."

"We'll need a bigger table," Gordon said as he started for the larger booth in the corner.

"Daddy doesn't like him."

"Shhh," Mary admonished.

"Here," Derek said as he placed Lindsey's food on his tray, "guess we're supposed to sit over there."

"Mary, Lindsey," Samantha said as she came up behind Derek, "leaving?"

"No," Mary answered, "Flash found a booth big enough for all five of us. Think we could just leave him there?"

"Mary, that's my associate you're so callously disparaging."

Derek slid into the booth, sitting on the small dirt imprint Lindsey's sneaker made. Samantha sat down next to him. Lindsey squirmed on his other side. "Let's see, Lindsey, your drink, and your hamburger, with one dainty bite out of the side."

"Where's my potato cake?" Lindsey asked, crawling up on Derek's knee to check out the tray.

"Here, Lindsey," her mother said, handing over one potato cake massacred by catsup. As everyone busied themselves applying sauces, Mary said, "So how's the investigation going?"

"First of all," Gordon said, "even if we were at liberty to talk about it, we'd never consider breaking the physician-patient confidentiality—"

"We're about three-quarters of the way through the autopsies, Mary." Samantha shook her head. "Never have I seen a bigger mess. Going back and forth between the lab and the temporary morgue is really a pain. Kate—"

"That's the receptionist," Gordon said to Derek.

"He knows Kate, *Eugene*," Mary said. "Go on, Sam."

Samantha pointed to Eugene. "By the way, there's a spare hand sitting on my desk. Bring it back to me when you go in to spot-check the pap smears."

"Maybe we can get a fingerprint. That would help."

"Gives new meaning to getting a helping hand." Derek pulled Lindsey down from the curtain. A smile touched his lips as he thought about the piggy bank she'd never see. The two pigs were royalty now, given a place of honor on either side of the fireplace in the living room.

"Lindsey, eat!" There was a lull in the conversation until Mary nodded and in a low voice said, "Look at the girl with Dean Curtis. She's a checkout clerk at the grocery store. Wonder how she latched onto him?" To Derek, she added, "He's the richest man in town."

"Probably sits on his face," Eugene said as he strained to see the girl. Derek was tempted to turn around, but instead watched Mary and Samantha break up.

"Does your wife have you trained, or what?" Mary winked at Samantha.

"More likely, Eugene," Samantha said, "it's the other way around."

Derek turned around slowly to have a look at the old man and the young girl. She didn't look much younger than Tiffany Smith. Mary leaned over Eugene to pull a napkin out of the dispenser to wipe tears of laughter from her eyes. Eugene flushed a bright red as he took a big bite out of his sandwich.

"Thanks, Eugene. My face must be smeared black with mascara." Mary held out the blackened napkin and then started laughing anew.

Samantha snickered and held her side.

"If I'd known you three were going to be so . . . embarrassing," Derek said, "Lindsey and I would have sat somewhere else."

"Eat, Lindsey," Mary told her as she blew her nose and shook her head. "Sits on his face."

Samantha erupted into full-blown laughter. "I have to . . . get back to work."

Derek grabbed her arm. "You, too. Eat."

25

"Dinner's on the table if that's you, Samantha. If it's a burglar, I'll have to set another plate."

"It's just me," Samantha answered as she closed the front door and headed for the hall closet. "I'm not hungry, though."

"No need to shout," Derek said as he appeared in the hallway.

His arms felt so warm, Sam wanted nothing more than to collapse into them. "I'm going up to bed. Want to join me? I'll let you hold me until I snore."

"My luck! Old what's-his-name found a girl to sit on his face, I get one who just wants to snore."

"Eugene can be very obtuse when he sets his mind to it."

"Here," Derek said as he helped her out of the coat and hung it up. "Eat something first."

She let him guide her to the table. "Smells good," Sam said as she sat down and propped her head up with her hand.

"Boneless chicken breasts à la sour cream." He glided a warm loving hand across her shoulders. "Old family recipe."

"On your mother's side, I suspect."

He busied himself at the Jen-aire. Why had she mentioned that? She tried hard not to remind him of her relationship with his father. "Actually, it's a lie. I concocted it myself." He spooned the rice into a serving bowl, placed it on the table, and sat down. "I heard you ran the FBI agents off the road."

She didn't actually run them off the road, they just sort

of slipped while they were chasing her. How was she supposed to know they were good guys? They didn't bother to introduce themselves. "They weren't used to driving on black ice."

"Samantha . . ." He took a deep breath as if he had thought better of whatever he was going to say. "So why didn't you tell me?"

"About their accident?" she asked as she buttered a blueberry muffin.

"About Eugene."

"Tell you what?" The cat jumped up on her lap and licked the butter from her knife.

Derek threw the cat outside. "Why do you always have to be the one to take in strays?" She thought he still meant Eugene, not her Siamese cat. "Don't you have enough to worry about without have a partner—"

"—that's worse than dragging a dead deer uphill?" She watched the steam roll off the broccoli. This was nothing she wanted to discuss with Derek.

"So why do you keep him?"

"He wanted to practice here. How could I tell him he couldn't? It is, after all, a free country. Besides, he's not a bad pathologist. Just a little slow."

"Is that why Mary called him Flash?" Derek cut off a piece of chicken.

She was really too tired to banter with him. "Ken doesn't like him going to cores in the E.R. Says he freezes when he sees a live patient, then they have to stumble over him. What difference does it make? At least he shares call."

"Just that I get back here and find everything's deteriorated. Emil is drunk most of the time—"

"Some of the time—"

"The dogs—"

Sam looked around. She was so tired she hadn't even missed them. "Where are the dogs?"

Derek shook his head. "Haven't seen them. Your dad looked good this evening, though."

"Thanks for visiting him."

"He enjoyed his dinner. Loved the pickled beets."

"Thank you, Derek." She was glad Derek cared. The nurse's assistants didn't spend enough time feeding her dad. He looked so thin the last time she visited. Why did she fight Derek at every turn? He was right about everything, and she knew he had only her welfare in mind. So why was she so irritated? "Derek, I'm sorry I've been such a bitch."

"You must have me confused with the FBI, I never called you that." He squeezed her hand softly. "And considering the strain you're under I'd say you've been a sweetheart."

"Well, I wouldn't go that far. Speaking about sweethearts, how's Tiffany?"

Derek gave her the sign that he was swallowing. "Found out the name of her first husband. Alan Martin."

"He's not her brother?"

"The Alan Martin who graduated from medical school in the sixties, Doyle's golf partner. Fingerprints at both the Eastside Clinic and the red-headed kid's apartment turned up the name Sean MacCade. Now guess what Tiffany's maiden name was."

"MacCade?"

He reached over and gave her a kiss. "You have the makings of a detective after all."

"She kills her first husband, has her brother impersonate him. Her second husband figures it out, she kills him."

"Who kills the brother in your supposition?"

"She does?"

He shook his head. "No, his death was a shock to her. And I understand she's doing some serious drinking to compensate for her loss."

Sam hadn't for a moment believed she was mourning Doyle. Who did kill the brother? "Anything else?"

"The toxicology test showed cyanide." He held out his hands as if waiting for applause. She duly clapped.

He scooted back his chair and patted his knees. That was all the invitation she needed. She climbed up on his lap and kissed him. "That's more like it." He managed to lift her from his lap and back into her own chair. "She's making late-night calls to a woman who works at the Westside Family Planning Center in Denver."

The chair was cold. She wrestled to straighten out her dress. Another abortion clinic. She wished they had a clue as to what was in Doyle's letter. "Does the woman drive a black Lexus?"

"Her name's not on the list, which I placed on the desk in the den for your inspection."

"What have you heard about the typewriter cartridge?"

"Transcription's in the mail, but it didn't sound like anything we're looking for."

"What kind of stuff?"

"Business letters. One to his broker, one to the IRS about an audit, one to his accountant about the audit, one to a cleaner's demanding payment for a ruined suit jacket. And one to Tiffany in St. Thomas."

"What did that one say?"

"He missed her, hoped she was having a good time and wasn't taking in too much sun. Finished?" Derek asked as he started to clear the table.

"Here, let me—"

"No, I'll clean up. Why don't you get ready for bed? I'll join you before you have a chance to nod off."

"Where do you think the dogs are?" She stared out the sliding door but saw only the dark forms of the patio furniture. "Hope the coyotes don't get them."

Derek slipped up behind her and wrapped his arms around her. "They're big boys. Don't worry. Oh . . . almost forgot." He took her hand and led her into the living room where Santa had made an early visit.

"What have you done?" She sat on the couch and tore through the largest of the gaily wrapped packages. "This is my lucky day. First Eugene brings me a hand in a shoe box and now—" It was a wintergreen-and-burgundy flowered dress with a black velvet collar. "You shouldn't have bought it."

She ripped through the next one to find another beautiful tent dress in navy blue with gold metallic threads forming diamond patterns on the bodice and gold stripes to the hem. As she unwrapped an ivory-and-gray corduroy number she felt her barrette loosen and fall away, and then a light hand combed through her hair, easing it down her back. "You shouldn't have bought them."

"You needed maternity clothes. What few you did possess went up in flames."

She didn't possess them, they were Mary's. She bet these would circulate widely among her friends after she was through with them. Eugene's wife first. "But I didn't need Paris creations," she whispered as she felt his lips tickling her shoulder.

"No, you would have settled for a K-Mart Blue Light Special, but you'll wear them for me."

A little box contained Tiffany's perfume. Derek dabbed some behind each of her ears and then on her wrists. He took her hands and pulled her up. "It smells irresistibly sensuous on you."

"And on Tiffany?" she asked, nuzzling against him.

"Smelled like flowers." He handed her one of the dresses to hold up and twirled her so she could see her image in the glass of the French door. "You're so beautiful," he whispered as his hands moved across her back, working out the knots in her aching muscles.

The dress slid to the carpet as her fingers traced down the outside of his thighs along the seams of his jeans.

He moved closer, gentle hands cupping her breasts. "Derek, I'm so glad you're back."

He nibbled at her ear. "Me, too."

Sam's senses reeled as his lips teased the line of her neck. A raging desire swept through her. "Couldn't you . . . leave the dishes?"

Derek pulled away suddenly, and stepped in front of her. "What do you suppose he wants?" He opened the French doors. "Emil?"

Only now did she see the figure coming toward them. Embarrassment drove her back; he must have seen them. Emil stepped inside, tracking mud on the carpet. He stared, glassy-eyed. She'd hear about his drinking again, if she knew Derek. "What is it, Emil?"

"It's the bison that's about to calve out. Think something's wrong."

"I'll go change. Wait here." Sam hurried upstairs and wiggled into a pair of jeans, and pulled them up over her bottom, never intending to zip them. She dragged her old baggy fisher-knit sweater off the shelf, then yanked boot-socks over swollen ankles before she twisted into her cowboy boots. Sam felt like she was walking on stilts as she started down the stairs, and hoped Derek wouldn't notice how high the heels were.

Derek, already wearing a hat and coat, stood at the bottom of the stairs holding hers. He helped her on with her parka, and then mashed the stocking cap over her hair and ears as she slipped on gloves.

"Get the flashlight out of the drawer next to the phone, I'll go back up for the Vaseline just in case."

Derek stopped her. "I'll get the Vaseline, you get the flashlight."

They stepped into the darkness, the wind howling around them. "Where is she, Emil?"

"Up against the near fence, by the barn," the unsteady Emil yelled over the wind.

Thank goodness for small favors. She didn't dare get on a horse these days and the four-wheeler wasn't much better.

The flashlight, moving over the bison cow that was lying down, showed one scrawny leg sticking out from under the tail. "What are you going to do, Samantha?"

"Here, hold the flashlight, I'll look for the other leg." She started to remove her coat.

"Wrong! You keep holding the flashlight and I'll look for the other leg." Derek ripped off his coat and rolled up his sleeves. "Is the Vaseline for me or her?"

"You. Here, Emil, hold the flashlight." She unscrewed the lid and held the jar out to Derek. "A big glob will do ya'."

Spreading the lubricant, Derek dropped to one knee and inched toward the tail. "Now what?"

"Feel inside her . . . Both arms."

He greased the other arm. "Hope you appreciate this, Bessy." He tightened his arms, unfurling cords like taut piano wire, and leaned into Monahseetah, getting a swat of her tail for his effort. Sam grabbed the tail. "Now what?"

"Do you feel the other leg?"

"Think I put out its eyes. No, it's his nose." His arms drove farther into the animal. "Yes, it's twisted under."

"Straighten it out."

"Easy for you to say, Bessy's fighting me all the way. I'm not sure I can get beyond the little . . . there. Found his hoof. I think it's a hoof. I hope it's a hoof."

"It's the hoof, Derek. Now pull it toward you." The bison bellowed, throwing a string of mucus. Emil moved back out of the way, but Sam felt the full blow of her wrath. "Thank you, Monahseetah."

"Monah . . . seetah?" Derek asked as he tugged.

"Custer's Southern Cheyenne mistress."

"You let me call her Bessy all this time? No wonder she hasn't been cooperating."

Sam could think of another reason. "Emil, will you go get some towels?" then yelled to him as he started back to the house, "Dirty towels." No sense using clean ones.

"There, got it. Now what?"

"Pull with her next contraction."

"Monahseetah. You ran out of amino acids?"

"Well, after I named Curly after an Indian, I just kept it up. The amino acids are for the horses."

"And Roseola, the disease horse?" Why did she have to justify the animals' names? "There, girl, push again. Here's the head, Samantha."

Sam looked over his shoulder. "Push," she yelled to the bison as Derek pulled.

"The little fellow's squirming."

"They're slippery. The first human baby I ever delivered got away from me."

Derek pulled until he fell over backwards and the calf plopped out and splashed into a pool of blood and fluid. Sam pushed around him to clear the mucus and blood out of the calf's nose. "The liquid's warm," Derek remarked.

"Body temperature."

"What did you mean by 'got away from me'?"

"I dropped it," she said, feeling the tiny thumping of the calf's heart. "Aren't you interested, Monahseetah, in what you have here?" Sam looked around. "Where's Emil?" She got up and found Derek's coat and rubbed the calf down with it. "A dirty towel would have been superlative. Can you carry the little lady around and stick her under her mother's nose?"

"It's like picking up a greased pig." Derek hauled the calf around and sat her down. "What happened to the baby?"

"It bounced back . . . figuratively speaking."

"What did you do?"

"Became a pathologist. Now be quiet. Let them bond."

They watched Monahseetah nudge the calf softly. Then slowly, back feet first, Monahseetah rose and started licking the calf tentatively. Soon Monahseetah was cleaning the calf as only a mother could.

"Shall we go? Don't think we're needed now."

Derek's eyes were still trained on the pair, but it was too damned cold to stand around gawking.

"What's going to happen next?"

"The little lady will take a couple of false starts, then finally stand on wobbly legs. I've got to go in, I'm freezing. You stay if you want. Here," she said handing him the wet coat.

"Like I'm going to put this on now." He wiped his hands and arms on the gummy coat. "I feel like I should hose off before going inside."

"A shower. That's for sure." Sam nuzzled under his arm as they started to the house. Emil was just coming out. "Though I kind of like you dirty."

"I always suspected you were the type to like dirty men."

She wrapped her arms around him; she'd take the shower with him. "So . . . like being a rancher?"

26

"A NEW HAIRSTYLE, KATE?" Derek asked the hospital lab's receptionist. The conspicuous stench of cheap musk cologne mingled with the fragile fragrance of Samantha's perfume. Derek made a mental note to buy Kate a more appealing scent at his first opportunity.

Kate shook tight ringlets of brown hair. "Not too new. You just haven't been around awhile."

Not since she wore red hair puffed high, by virtue of a good deal of hairspray, which some sort of oil now replaced. "I like it."

"Really, you like it?" she asked, patting her hair. Her palm glistened with oily residues. "It's just like the pictures of the models in all those New York glamour magazines. Been a little hard for everyone around her to get used to . . . new ideas, you know."

Derek flashed a quick smile. "So . . . Samantha in her office?"

Kate raised a black-penciled brow. "Went off with Dr. Miller a while ago. Coffee, I think he said. Should've been back by now."

He headed toward her cubbyhole. "I'll be in her office."

"That's Dr. Gordon's office, now." She motioned to the battered metal desk across from her. "They brought this one up from the boiler room for Sam."

Derek took off his trench coat and sat behind the dilapidated desk. The cubbyhole was bad enough. It was so like his new wife to give Eugene her office, and so like her not to have mentioned it. Nor did it escape Derek's attention that she was out with Dr. Miller and it was Dr. Gordon's office. But she was just plain *Sam*.

He took scratch paper and pen and started a list of chores. "Is it worse now?"

Derek wondered how much work Samantha was able to accomplish sitting across from Kate. "Is what worse now?"

"The weather. Think it'll snow?"

He shrugged. "Cold enough. Might. Wish the wind would settle."

"This is nothing. You should see it down Laramie way. My husband once fell over when he got out of the camper one morning because he was leaning into the wind, and there wasn't any. Boy, was he surprised."

"Bet he was." On the way in, a harsh gust had whipped around the corner of the building and all but carried away the elderly woman ahead of him. Derek and she had walked the rest of the way into the hospital arm-in-arm.

"Heard you had a new buffalo last week."

Derek kneaded his right hand, remembering. It had ached for four days after the delivery, but he stopped complaining and held Samantha in awe for as many days after hearing the story of how she had to dismember a dead calf inside the mother in order to save the mother's life. Hard work, ranching.

"Goddammit, Skip, stick it up your ass. I'm not about to take it!"

Kate caught Derek's eye. "I think I hear Sam, now."

Derek smiled. "I believe you're right. It does indeed sound like my lovable wife's sweet little voice."

"Didn't sound so sweet to me. Wonder who she's yelling at?"

The mystery was solved as Samantha appeared with a uniformed police officer one step behind, waving a paper. Another speeding citation, Derek assumed. There was no mistaking the high flame on her beautiful cheekbones.

"They were in the city limits," the policeman told her as he thrust the folded paper toward her.

She stepped awkwardly aside and crossed downy arms

defiantly over magnificent breasts, so insatiably familiar. "I don't give a fuck if they both took a dump on the mayor's yard. I don't live in town and you can't give me that."

"What's the trouble, officer?" Derek asked as he stepped between them. Out of the corner of his eye he watched Kate spring from the room into the lab, which had gotten exceptionally quiet.

"Well . . . ah . . ." He pointed to Samantha, now sitting on the edge of her desk glaring at the policeman. "Her dogs were seen in Colony South, at Nineteenth and Colonial Drive."

"At Jeffrey's former house, he means. One of the neighbors thought one of them looked a little like Fido. Not that they've seen Fido since he was a pup." Her lab coat pulled tight across the protruding belly as she slid from the desk. She stabbed a finger against Skip's chest. "So the fucking police think that's proof enough to give me another ticket."

Derek pulled her back. "Did you apprehend the suspects, officer?"

Skip coughed, and then gave him a lopsided grin. "Well, they were gone by the time I arrived."

"When did this heinous crime allegedly take place?" Derek asked.

The policeman opened the citation and cleared his throat. "At two-thirty-seven P.M., November eighteenth."

The day after he delivered the buffalo. The dogs had disappeared for three days before they turned up dirty and hungry. So they'd gone to town. "What would you say if I told you *our* two dogs haven't been out of my sight for a month?" Samantha's head whipped around. He could feel her emerald eyes burning through him and only hoped she would wait until the man was gone before laying into him. He reached up under her lab coat and gently massaged the sides of her abdomen. The baby was kicking up a storm, adding to her irritation, no doubt.

Skip carefully folded the citation. "I . . ." he cleared his throat again, "I guess there's been a little mistake."

Samantha started to take a step forward, but Derek drew her back. "My wife and I appreciate your consideration in this matter."

Skip nodded as he took a step back. "Well . . . I guess . . ." He looked over his shoulder as if he had something more important to take care of. "I really should—"

"We know how busy you are with all the Federal investigators coming and going. Samantha can identify with that, can't you, dear?" Derek hugged her, hoping her pursed lips would relax a little. They didn't.

"Yes, yes," Skip said as he backed into the hall. "I need to get back." He gave a little wave of apology.

He had no sooner disappeared before Samantha pushed away. "You lied," she whispered hoarsely.

"No, I simply asked him what he'd say if I told him that." Derek shrugged. "Was it my fault he misinterpreted the question?" Her eyes were narrow slits with the tiniest glint of green. "I wish you could see your face."

"Don't be patronizing!" She swung around the desk and sat down hard. "So what if the dogs were in town? I live in the country where there are no leash laws."

"*We* live in the country. Apparently it doesn't matter. They wouldn't have issued the citation otherwise. They do know the ordinances, my dear." A husky groan escaped Samantha's throat for what Derek considered an inordinate period of time. He proceeded with clinical caution. "Now, Samantha, not to change the subject, but . . . do you have your driver's license?" Her face told him he was adding injury to insult and went on quickly. "Now that you have all the victims identified, I'm taking you on your honeymoon."

Samantha threw her arms in the air. "Just wonderful. I'm swamped, and you want me to go gallivanting off somewhere."

"To the Caribbean. Didn't you always want to spend Thanksgiving on the Love Boat?"

"Gee, Derek, I lay awake at nights wishing I could spend

Thanksgiving on the Love Boat." She picked up a pencil and stabbed it through her blotter, sending the lead flying. He bet she went through an awful lot of pencils.

Derek waited for Kate to sit back down at her desk and get comfortable. She took out a piece of typing paper and rolled it into the typewriter. "At two this afternoon you and I are getting on the plane."

Samantha threw the pointless pencil across her desk. "Is that an order?"

"It's an invitation." He looked around, noticing that Kate hadn't started typing. "Where's Dr. Gordon? Thought he was taking Thanksgiving call so he could go to Utah over Christmas."

"He's over at the VA. We have too much to do. I can't go, Derek."

Derek sighed. "A pity. Tiffany and I'll speak of you kindly."

"Tiffany?" A glint flickered in her eyes. He had her interest now. She casually leaned her palms on the desk and, glancing at Kate, smiled. "Tiffany's going with us?"

"She's already there."

"Really?" Samantha's voice sounded exceedingly pleasant for a change. "I'd hate missing the chance to see Tiffany again. How long would we be away?"

"Back Sunday night. You'll only miss tomorrow and Wednesday."

The corners of her lips turned up. "How much work could there be the day before a holiday?"

Derek shrugged. "Probably enough for only one pathologist."

She nodded. "Probably so."

"So—all you need is your driver's license. I've got your birth certificate right here." He patted his breast pocket. Turning to Kate, he said, "She doesn't look fifty-two."

Kate giggled.

"Ha-ha. Very funny." Samantha glanced at her watch. "I've got a million things to do before the plane leaves. I need to tell Eugene, pack, tell Emil, go to the nursing home, tell Daisy."

"All you have to do is meet me at the airport, I'll take care of everything else. Kate, please tell Eugene and tell him to call the billing office and tell Daisy." He turned back to Samantha. "See how easy that was? I'll drop by the nursing home and check up on your dad, then go home and pack for both of us. I'll talk to Emil, though we had a nice long chat just the other day. You *do* have a driver's license, don't you, my darling?"

Samantha glared at him, and then leaned over and pulled out the bottom drawer. "Here," she said, throwing her wallet across the desk, "see for yourself."

"Nice picture, wouldn't you say, Kate?" Derek made certain it wasn't expired, and then rounded the desk to give her a kiss on the cheek. "It's a nice picture," he said, placing it in her hand. He turned back when he reached the door. "By the way, do you have a preference of kennels? Or should we pick the dogs up at the city pound on Monday?"

27

"SAMANTHA, CAN YOU do something for me?"

She turned an eye to Derek, but unless she moved her head off his shoulder, she wouldn't see much more than the black stubbles on his cheek. "Depends. If you want me to sleep, I'll force myself."

"Could you go over to a slot machine and play for a while?"

It was hot and humid and Sam hated Puerto Rico already. She pushed herself upright on the white leather couch along the walkway between the bustling casino and the quiet bar. "Couldn't I go downstairs to the reception counter and get a room? Even if it's just for a couple of hours?"

Derek stroked her sticky arm, placing her at his mercy. "I know you're tired, sweetheart, but we don't have a couple of hours. Need to talk to someone for a minute, eat breakfast, take you on a quick sight-seeing tour of the island, and then head for the ship. You can sleep all afternoon in the cabin. Round the clock if you wish."

"Don't think talking to someone for a minute missed my attention, but why do you feel the need to show me San Juan?" Sam trembled, feeling his mouth tease her neck. It was not altogether fair play on his part. "What's to see? Thought everyone from Puerto Rico moved to New York."

"Need to visit El Morro this morning." He rose and gave her a hand up. "Come on, I'll get you a roll of quarters."

"What was that first part again?" Sam asked, stretching the soreness from her shoulders.

"El Morro?" Derek threw their coats over his shoulder. Should have stashed them in a locker when they went through the Denver airport. "The fortress that protected San Juan from pirates like Sir Francis Drake."

"Pirates? Drake a pirate? That's not what my fourth grade social studies book said."

"Then you didn't go to school in San Juan, Spain, or New York." He took her elbow. "Come on."

"Oh, Derek," she whined. He was in his element; she was dead tired and wanted to go home.

"And later, if you're a real good girl I'll show you a leper colony."

Sam wondered what a modern leper colony would be like. That would be worth seeing. She'd be a real good girl. Armed with a roll of quarters, she sat down at a poker machine between two middle-aged women. Going by the black-beaded dress on the dark-haired lady on her left, they were left over from last night's gamblers. That and a tray filled to the rim with quarters. Sam put in a quarter and pushed the Deal button absently, her eyes on Derek as he went into the bar. The woman at her left said something to her excitedly, which the woman on her right seemed to answer in quick Spanish. Sam smiled and nodded, wishing she'd studied Spanish in school instead of Latin. Both women pointed to the cards on her screen. She looked the cards over but didn't see why they were making such a fuss. She saved the king and pushed the Deal button. Both women groaned and stared at her as if she were an idiot.

Not speaking the language was frustrating her again. Not that she'd had one moment of peace from frustration since she went to that damned convention in San Diego. They—or at least she; Derek kept his cards close to his chest most of the time, to add to her frustration—still had no idea what was going on. Whatever it was, it was big enough to kill Dr. Smith and Tiffany's brother, bomb a family planning clinic and a plane.

She looked at the new hand. Two sevens, a queen, an ace, and a ten. She punched the Hold buttons under the sevens. The women groaned. What was she doing wrong now? Sam absently pushed on the little foot stretching against her ribs. "Find another place!" she said almost under her breath.

"Oh, you speak English!" the woman at her right exclaimed. "Look," she pointed to the top of the machine, "see where it says $178,558? You have to put five quarters in to play for it."

"Five quarters," Sam parroted.

"And see this," the other woman added, pointing to the payoffs for the different hand combinations, "you had a flush last hand."

All five cards in the same suit, she read, wishing she'd sat down in front of one of the machines with all the fruit.

Sam counted as she dropped five coins in the machine and watched the big number light up. A dollar and a quarter to play each hand! She could go to the matinee for two pulls and be entertained for two hours. She hoped Derek would hurry up.

The roll of quarters gone and her fingers black, Sam watched the women play. In contrast to her stumbling ways, they had it down to a science.

"Ready to go?" Derek asked, sneaking up behind her.

"Yes, and I was a very good girl. Now you can take me to the leper colony."

"I said I'd show you the leper colony. I never promised to take you to it." Derek gave her a hand up. "You know, there's something we need to discuss now that you're not preoccupied with work."

That wasn't fair. She'd wasted ten dollars and she didn't get to visit a leper colony?

Derek turned his attention to the woman in black and spoke in rapid Spanish. From the laughter of both women, Sam suspected she was the butt of their joke.

"What do we need to talk about, my darling?"

"Now, now." Derek picked up her purse and took her by the arm. "Don't jump all over me. I've been very busy while you've been playing poker."

Sam craned her neck to look around at him. It wasn't easy being mad at a smiling man. She sighed and marched wearily along. After they were seated in the restaurant Sam asked again, "What do we need to discuss now that I'm away from work?"

Derek looked up from the menu. "What would you like?"

Sam looked at the Spanish menu. "Surprise me."

"We need to discuss the plans for the addition to the house."

"Okay, let's discuss it. What are we going to build on?"

"Two bedrooms, for starters. You have one spare bedroom. In order to bring your father home, we'll need a round-the-clock nurse. And then we need a nursery. That's three rooms. Assuming the nurse is willing to do a little babysitting on the side. Otherwise we need four."

"I thought you said you were going to be the baby's caretaker."

"Didn't I say a *little* babysitting? You know, Saturday afternoons. Not all movies are rated G."

"Bring my father home? He likes the company at the nursing home."

"*Liked.* He's beyond that. He needs to be with us now." He made her feel guilty about the spotty attention she had been paying her father of late.

"Did you find out anything new about Tiffany?"

"No, you don't. Home improvement is the subject."

"Seems like home improvement—" Derek squeezed her hand to silence her as the waiter approached. After he'd left with whatever order Derek had given him, she went on. "What did you find out when you talked to whomever in the bar?"

"Mary offered a bassinet, but said we'd want to get the baby out of our room as soon as possible."

"Derek! Will you talk to me, please?"

"I won't know anything definite until after El Morro. If we don't get started right away we'll have to wait until spring."

He could add a castle with a moat around it for all she cared. "Whatever takes your fancy tickles me pink."

Derek grinned. "All right, I'll tell them we want the nursery painted pink."

"This is it?" Sam asked as she looked around their cabin. "First you show me a dot of buildings you say is a leper colony and now you bring me here?" Two single beds hugged opposite walls, the distance between the beds about the width of the two suitcases that had been placed in their room. The tiny bathroom had a shower instead of a bath. Two royal blue chairs and a small lampstand lined the left side of the cabin, while a dresser ran between the foot of one bed and the door to the bathroom.

"Actually, Samantha, this is one of the larger staterooms." Derek closed the door behind him. "And it was the best one I could get on short notice. Most people plan their vacations well in advance."

Sam watched him throw the suitcases on the bed to the left. She tossed her purse on the other bed, staking her claim. "Doesn't look like the rooms on the Love Boat, that's for sure. But I'll be happy just to lie down." No sooner were the words out of her mouth than she felt the zipper down her back give way, his mouth teasing the nape of her neck. "Can we talk about Tiffany now?"

"Raise your arms," he said as he brought the dress up over her head. "All we know is that Tiffany was seen going into a private clinic on St. Thomas."

"But she wasn't seen leaving?"

"Nor was a messenger from the Westside Family Planning Clinic, who showed up at the St. Thomas clinic with an ice chest of human tissue."

She sat down on the bed. The pieces were starting to fall

into place. "What kind of patients is this private clinic catering to?"

"Very rich ones."

"Diabetics?" Yes, that was it. Fetal tissue.

"What's the smile for?"

She waved for him to be quiet while she thought it through. "Okay, this is my theory. They're using fetal tissue from abortion clinics. They must be isolating the islet cells, which produce insulin, and surgically implanting the cells into the diabetic's pancreas."

"That's illegal in the U.S.?"

"Not so much illegal as unethical or immoral, depending on your viewpoint. You know, the abortion dispute. That would explain the bombing of the abortion clinic in LA and Tiffany's brother's death."

"And what of Doyle and his letter?"

"Maybe he'd gotten wind of a pro-life terrorist group's plan to bomb the clinic and was killed for trying to stop it. I don't know. Would pro-lifers really kill a plane full of people? That part doesn't make sense."

"Don't jump to conclusions about the plane crash. There was a drug courier on board."

She noticed he opened the porthole so he wouldn't have to look at her while he lied. She'd overheard him on the phone saying that she wasn't to be told that the explosive devices used in both bombings were bought from the same wholesaler. At least not until the baby came. And she would pretend not to feel guilty about the forty-eight deaths she had caused, if it would keep him from worrying about her.

"So why the boat, Derek? Why didn't we fly into St. Thomas?"

"Tomorrow when we dock in St. Thomas we'll be taking on three patients from the clinic. It's all part of the package. You can try out your theory on them."

"Good, I can sleep today." Sam crawled into bed.

He took a black traveling case from his suitcase. Sam stretched out on the bed and watched him run his electric shaver over the stubble on his handsome face.

"Samantha?" She heard him through a fog of sleep. "Do you want me to wake you for lunch?"

"Aren't you going to sleep?" she may have asked aloud.

"Have to check seating arrangements for our meals. We don't want to sit with just anyone. Here, let's get these off. You won't need stockings this trip."

Sam turned on her side and surrendered to sleep.

▽

28

Sam THREW BACK the covers; the air was stuffy, the room close. It took a minute for her to realize where she was. Her bed at home was so much more comfortable than this narrow one. What kind of honeymoon is it if you can't fall asleep in your husband's arms? And her morning sickness was back. She'd almost forgotten the feeling.

She tried to sit up but fell back on her pillow as her head reeled. The room continued to wobble. Back and forth the room swayed. It wasn't her, the room was literally swaying. It was the boat and she was seasick. She never felt like this on John's catamaran. This was so unfair.

Sam forced herself up and dragged into the bathroom. It wasn't any better there, but she did find her cosmetic bag. She rummaged through it to see if she had some Dramamine or Compazine. She ended up pulling out a scopolamine patch. She was going into her eighth month of pregnancy; the drug wouldn't cause congenital defects now, she assured herself as she stuck the patch behind her ear. It would be a couple of hours before it took effect. She had to get to the center of the ship. The trick was to get to the deck and look at the horizon.

Where were the clothes she'd been wearing?

The suitcases were gone. Mr. Tidy must have put everything away while she was conked out. She groped toward the closet door, feeling the pitch and roll of the ship. She had to get dressed, she had to get on top. She had to lie down. No, she had to get out of there.

She wasn't impressed with the selection of clothes Derek had packed. The outfits he'd brought back from Europe were for winter. She ripped the blue plaid dress off the hanger. Who cared that she'd worn it all day yesterday and last night and that it was a wrinkled mess? She only wanted to be dressed and out of the cabin.

The *Poseidon* passengers had nothing on her. She didn't actually know which floor was which, but it didn't matter. As long as she kept climbing, she'd eventually be topside.

She fell behind a couple in swimwear and followed them out onto a deck. There a three-piece band played the theme to "The Love Boat." Fast friends talked and laughed and sipped drinks at small tables around the pool; cocktail waitresses milled about. Sam saw a couple of empty lounge chairs on the upper terrace. She climbed the spiral stairs, not caring that the wind had puffed her dress and everyone around the pool knew she wore boring white panties.

Sam eased herself into the first empty lounge chair, between two little girls. It felt wonderful to have something supporting her whirling head. She kept her eyes on the horizon and tried not to referee the tug-of-war over a bottle of suntan lotion.

She watched the edge of the world until it blurred like the voices around her.

"Samantha?"

She stirred to Derek's gentle shake.

"I've been looking all over for you." Derek tried to hide his cigarette behind his back. "What are you doing up here?"

"Derek, I'm seasick." She looked around to find the loud girls gone, replaced by a couple of senior citizens. "I had to get out of the cabin."

He took a last drag from his cigarette and pitched it over the railing. He sat on the foot of her chair and lifted her skirt. "You need to get out of the sun, your legs are beet-red. How long have you been here?"

Sam hoisted a leg. It was crimson to the bottom of her knee and white as a sheet from there up. "Long enough."

She should have asked the girls to rub her down.

Derek rose and held out his hand. "Let's get you inside."

Sam absently rubbed the patch behind her ear as she watched the dining room fill.

She shifted to see where Derek had disappeared to. It was embarrassing sitting at a table for eight alone. Alone, if no one counted the waiter and his two helpers standing over her. It hadn't taken long to figure out where the other couples were. They, no doubt, were on St. Thomas. She looked up at the waiter. "What?"

"Señora?" the tall, thin, sallow man asked as he leaned over her shoulder. His black hair was slicked back like a Chicago mobster. Perhaps that was why she was so intimidated by him.

"Oh, I'm sorry. I thought you were talking to me." She couldn't hear, either. And her legs throbbed. She wished she hadn't let Derek talk her into coming down for dinner.

The waiter pointed to one of his helpers and spoke in what Sam decided was Italian. She'd heard someone refer to the dining room personnel as the Roman Army. Practically everyone who worked on the ship was English, except the dining room staff. The helper placed a roll on one of the many plates in front of her. "Have you decided, Señora?"

Sam opened the international-theme menu again. The English translation was too small to read without her glasses. Her glasses were in the bottom of her purse somewhere, but she didn't have the energy to bend over and dig them out. She chose the course of least resistance. She pointed.

"Penne all'arrabbiata." He kissed the tips of his fingers. "Very good."

She closed the menu.

He opened it. "Appetizer? The fruit cup with lemon sherbet perhaps?"

"Yes, the fruit cup."

"Soup?"

Sam shook her head. There was nothing she liked less than eating in a restaurant alone. She twisted around, but didn't see Derek anywhere.

"Salad, Señora? Salade champenoise. Very good."

"All right."

"Dressing?"

"Blue cheese."

"Roquefort," he said as he wrote.

"Roquefort," she parroted.

"Señor?"

Derek slipped into his chair. He opened his menu. "Escargots bourguignonne, Soupe à l'oignon, Croutons au fromage, Entrecote de boeuf sautée au poivre vert, Salade champenoise . . . roquefort."

"Roquefort," the waiter repeated as he wrote.

"Roquefort," Sam parroted.

"What does the sommelier suggest tonight?" Derek inspected the wine list. "Chablis Wente."

Sam felt the waiter tug the menu out from under her arm. Her eyes remained riveted on Derek. "He thinks I'm a fool, you know."

"No, he doesn't."

"I said blue cheese."

$\triangledown$

29

THE SUBCUTANEOUS EDEMA caused by yesterday's nap in the sun made her feet and ankles look like thick tree stubs. And Sam didn't know which was worse, motion sickness or blurred vision, a side effect of the scopolamine. Things kept going from bad to worse, and she wondered how Derek put up with her whining.

So far she didn't have any complaints about St. Thomas, though they hadn't left the dock. She dug her swollen toes into the thongs Derek bought in the ship's store after she discovered that her shoes fit as well as the glass slipper fit Cinderella's stepsisters. She smoothed out the wintergreen-and-burgundy dress and gave the black velvet collar a tug to line up the points. It was uncomfortably warm under the beating sun, but she wasn't about to complain.

Her fellow passengers were gaily tromping down the gangplank, milling around the dock, and queuing up for the sightseeing vans. Sam sat quietly on the bench and pretended she could see them. They should have gotten on the first van when they had their chance, but Derek pulled her back and parked her on the bench.

Now he was nowhere to be seen—even if she could see anything.

"Here's a present for the loveliest woman in the world," Derek said as he slipped up and sat down beside her and handed over a large green sack.

"So why are you giving it to me?" She threw it down on top of Derek's camera equipment.

Derek reached around her. "Sounds like a twang of self-pity to me." He opened the sack and pulled out a white gauze sundress with colorful ribbons like the ones the waitresses in the Mexican restaurant wore, except the material was gathered at the yoke instead of the waist.

"Where'd you get this?"

"From the shopping complex behind this fence. You know, the building that looks like a big concrete warehouse from this side." He rose and gathered up their belongings. "There's also a ladies' room. Do you want to change?"

Sometimes it pays not to complain.

The sundress was so lightweight she barely knew she had anything on. She figured everyone could see through it, but didn't care. Derek took a long pull of his cigarette and crushed it under foot the moment she came back. He turned down a crinkled piece of the satin ribbon that was sewn along the seam about midleg, where the ruffle fell almost to her ankles.

"Your eyes are dilated," he said as he took the winter dress from her. "What's wrong?"

"It's the scopolamine. Everything's blurry." She ripped off the patch behind her ear. "Guess I'd rather be seasick."

"Here, wear my sunglasses." He wrapped an arm around her. "Come on, Woods is waiting."

Woods turned out to be the black-as-coal driver of the gray-and-red van, and the king of platitudes, all delivered in rapid-fire calypso lilt. They were the last to board the van and sat in front with the driver.

"When you drive with Woods be patient so you won't be a patient in the hospital tomorrow. It isn't what you do it's how you do it, so keep your head on and your brain inside it. Laugh and the world laughs with you, cry and you cry alone. We drive on the left side of the street, we drive on the left side of the street."

One of the two pubescent cherubs behind them kicked the back of the seat to the tune of the heavy metal music that pounded out of his earphones. Derek put a stop to that by grabbing his leg.

Woods turned Sam's head so she could see the Danish flag somewhere on the hillside above the tangle of vines or whatever the green was. She was looking in the right direction now. The Danes wouldn't give up the dock area when the Americans bought St. Thomas, so now they were landlords or something, a piece of useless knowledge to inflict on Kate.

"We'll go over to Coral Wall and be underwater, but I guarantee you won't be wet. The island is twelve miles long, and four-and-a-half miles wide." Kate was going to love that little tidbit. "Our population is fifty thousand. Our economy is tourism. You are our bread and butter. We will not kill the goose that lays the golden egg.

"Look to the left. There's our one-flavor ice cream store. Then Woolworth, and a supermarket, the IRS building. To the right is the hospital. Left, McDonald's for your Big Mac."

The winding road added to Sam's misery and she was relieved when they arrived at Coral World, not Coral Wall.

A mocha-skinned girl wearing a red-and-white-flowered sleeveless dress started her lecture as soon as they reached the entrance. She pointed out the different buildings and was telling them what time they were to meet back at the van when Derek pulled Sam away, parked her on the stone wall near a bird cage about the size of their spare bedroom, and took off to parts unknown.

She watched what she thought was a huge chameleon scamper across the dirt. A man played some sort of calypso music on both a keyboard and a big metallic drum. The caged birds squawked in violent disapproval. A chameleon of another kind sauntered toward her, carrying a broad-brimmed straw hat. She might have known he was on another mercy run.

"Like it?" he asked, dropping it on her head. "The woman in the shop said you're supposed to tie it down with a colorful scarf." He pulled a long scarf out of his sleeve and worked his magic. "Anyone ever tell you you wear a hat well?"

"Thousands of admirers."

He pulled her up and bent under the hat for a kiss. "Shall we see if Woods is right?" She must have looked at him questioningly. "About his guarantee that we won't be wet."

"This is all well and good, Derek, but why don't we go to the clinic? I can explain that I'm a doctor and thought I'd visit while I was in town. Any fool would know that means I'm writing off part of the trip as a business expense."

"And what would you do if someone showed up in your lab?"

"I'd do the same as I do with the scout troops and school classes. I'd march them over to the blood bank and show them my blood supply."

He felt his cigarettes, but thought better of bringing them out. "And what if you run into Tiffany?"

She didn't have an answer for that one.

"You'll have your chance with the patients at dinner."

"If they've just had surgery, they won't be at dinner. I guarantee it."

Derek gave her a wait-and-see look and guided her off.

They weren't wet. The round room with portholes was straight out of *Twenty-thousand Leagues under the Sea.* "Shark, shark, tuna, shark, eel," Derek said as they looked out a porthole at the coral water.

"Which is the eel?"

"It's gone." He took her hand and led her to the next window. "No, it's gone. Shark, shark—"

"Don't, Derek. People will think I'm retarded."

"Or blind." He gave her a reassuring squeeze. "The one in Auckland is best. You stand on a conveyor belt and glide through a glass tunnel."

"You and the children can bring home pictures."

"Better chance of having children if we stay together. Let's go upstairs and sit down."

They sat at a table with a fiftyish couple from Woods's van. The woman, Betsy, was a kindergarten teacher from Canada, they eventually learned; the man, Conrad, didn't actually say what he did for a living. Nor did Derek. He just said they owned a ranch in Wyoming.

"What's in Wyoming?" Betsy asked in a soft voice, "cattle or sheep?"

"We have bison on our ranch," Sam said. "Buffalo."

"Really? Is there . . . do you . . . you raise them for food, hey?" the woman asked.

Sam shifted and pushed the baby away from her ribs. He had a one-track mind. "No, they're pets."

Betsy turned to Derek. "How do you make the ranch pay?"

"We don't." A devilish hand crawled up Sam's thigh; she sipped her ginger ale.

"Beautiful here, hey?"

Sam nodded to Betsy, and then stared out the glass wall to the bay. "So many different shades of blue."

Derek looked at his watch. "Drink up. Woods is await'n." He picked up her purse and hat, and then pulled her up.

Having to continually rise from under a bowling ball was one thing. Having swollen feet, no ankles, and a sunburn stretched tight over ballooning legs was downright impossible. "You know why I love you?" she whispered to Derek. "Because you haven't ditched me."

Their next stop was at Bluebeard's castle—of late, a hotel. Woods gathered everyone round the old cannons. Sam leaned back against Derek's chest. Why hadn't she stayed on board ship?

Woods pointed toward the tree-covered hillside. "There is the highest point on the island, fifteen hundred forty-seven feet high. And over there is the Danish flag where our ship is tied up." Sam still didn't see it, but kept following his finger as he continued his rapid-fire speech. "The long white building is the Virgin Island Hotel. The Virgin Island Hotel. The governor lives in the red roof house over there." All the buildings had red roofs. "And over there is the free hotel. When you get back home you tell your friends that Woods showed you a free hotel. Know what a free hotel is? A prison. You eat, drink, and sleep and don't cost you anything."

Everyone laughed.

Sam laughed. What the hell, she wanted to be a good sport.

"Look behind you. Bluebeard's castle where he killed seven wives. But like I tell you. If a man has a wife you know what you have and don't know what you're going to get so better to hold on to what you have."

Derek gave her a reassuring hug.

"We go to the lily pond then the castle, then you go inside and do your own thing. Woods will give you a time, not yet, to meet back."

The group followed Woods to the lily pond where Sam sat down on the edge. The two boys were fighting over the headset. She wished she could have some of their excess energy.

Woods leaned over and stirred the oily water, moving the lilies. "As Jackie Gleason says, 'How sweet it is.' So now we leave the lily pond and go into the castle."

"Hardly worth sitting," Derek said as he helped her up.

In the circular room of the stone ruin Woods said, "Thick and strong. Thick and strong." He pointed to a sign next to the door leading into a garden. "They don't like us to take guest beyond this point. Woods will give you fifteen minutes. Fifteen minutes and then that's the last train. All right?"

"Let's see if we can find a seat inside. Would you like to sit down for fifteen minutes?"

"I should have skipped the tour of the castle and gone right inside. Let's make the ladies' room our first stop."

Sam came out of the rest room only to discover that she'd misplaced Derek again. A quick scan of the empty white lobby made her wonder if she'd missed the last train. Then she saw the group milling around in the little shops off to her left.

In the window was a voodoo doll. She had read somewhere that voodoo was actually a religion embracing good spirits, that the sacrificing was to appease the evil forces. Maybe she should get a couple to replace the pigs Amy and Lindsey didn't get. Probably not. Mary and Ken might not approve, and no one in Amy's family was speaking to her.

She found Derek inside the shop at the perfume counter. "I hope you're not buying that for me."

"Smell," he said, holding out his wrist. "Like it better than Kate's?"

"I like the smell of formaldehyde better than Kate's cologne."

He winked at the girl behind the counter. "This one." He dropped the sack into her purse as they were leaving. "You'll see that it finds its way out of there and into Kate's hands?"

"It will be my pleasure."

"You won't forget?"

"One whiff of her musk and I'll remember."

"Time to head back. Last train, you know."

Woods made one more stop on their way back to the ship. Sam sat in the van as everyone else filed out to get one last picture of the hillside and the harbor from the side of the cliff. "Come on out, let me take your picture," Derek said as he shifted his camera to his left hand to offer her his right.

"Oh, Derek, I don't want my picture taken."

He wiggled his fingers. "Come on."

She pouted as she got out.

"Stand next to Woods."

Obligingly she skirted around the other picture-takers and replaced the heavyset—like she should call anyone else heavy—woman after she was finished being immortalized with the tour guide. Woods tucked her under his arm. "Smile big for the birdie."

After Derek snapped the shutter Sam started to walk away. Woods pulled her back. "He's not finished."

She looked around at him.

"Call out to your husband, Dr. Turner, tell him to take one more for your mother," he said quietly.

"Your accent's slipping."

"Call out to him."

"Derek, take another for my father." Out of the side of her mouth she added, "My mother's dead."

"I'm sorry."

"Is he taking a picture of something behind us?" she asked as she smiled big for the birdie.

Derek yelled out, "Here's one for the office."

"Can you see that pseudo-Spanish-style building with the red tile roof? Down the hill adjacent to Derek. That's the Blanca Institute."

It was all so bewildering and she hadn't seen anything he'd pointed out. She smiled broadly, and not for the picture Derek wasn't taking of them. "I never even saw the Danish flag."

He squeezed her and rattled off in his best calypso tongue something about herding up and heading out. "Last chance for snapshots with Woods."

30

"YOU COULD HAVE told me!" Samantha's lips smacked as she threw the hat and purse on her bed.

She was gorgeous when mad. The enchanting butterfly tattoo, as she deemed it, darkened to the deepest ruby. Perhaps Derek should keep her angry the rest of the trip; she bubbled with energy. "Why? Don't you have enough to worry about?"

"If you'd told me I could have acted better."

"You acted fine. You were wonderful. And natural. We looked just like a couple on holiday. The very pregnant wife and the worried husband—which is literally what we are—getting in one last vacation before we're strapped down with a family."

"Strapped down with a family?" Her eyes caught the light and flashed like perfect emeralds. "Is that what the baby means?"

"No. It didn't come out the way I meant it." He felt for his cigarettes. He'd give anything for one right now. "To other people who don't know how important the baby is to us, they would see it as one last chance to be alone. And how happy I am that we are alone right now."

"And what does that mean?"

"It means I wish we weren't having this fight. You could instead be curled in my arms resting up for dinner. Or I could be massaging . . . even kissing your feet. You know, enjoyable things like that."

She folded her arms over her chest, took a couple of steps to the porthole and looked out. "I'm sorry. It's just that I want to be your partner." She turned back, her face soft and vulnerable. "I want to be trusted. I don't want there to be any more secrets between us."

"Look Samantha. There are parts of your life that don't include me." He caught a glimpse of flaming anger.

"Like what?"

"Your work. I know you don't exclude me on purpose, and I wouldn't expect you to have to explain the reason why you order this or that test to solve a medical problem. You know what you're doing and I trust you to do your job as you see fit without consulting me. This is the same thing. I'm trying to do my job and I don't want to stop and explain everything. I'm not qualified to be your partner in medicine and you're not qualified to be mine."

She'd reached the bathroom by the time he'd finished. She pirouetted. "End of lecture?"

"No," he answered, inching closer. He wanted to touch her, hold her, make her understand. "I've given you what's good . . . my whole heart and soul. Leave me to deal with the trash. Let me protect you from it."

She had no sooner melted into his arms before she was pulling away. "Shit! They're moving the boat."

"Lecture Number Two—must you talk like a common sailor?"

Samantha slapped her menu down on top of Derek's. "I'm having whatever you're having."

He opened the menu. "Shall I have lobster or prime rib?" He didn't give Samantha a chance to answer. "I believe our dinner companions are starting to arrive. The ball's in your court once they're here. *Partner.*" Following the maître d' was an elderly couple, who Derek suspected hailed from Texas if he could go by the big man's western bolo, cowboy shirt, jeans, boots, well-worn Stetson, and wild white sideburns. The petite woman on his arm was wearing a coral squaw dress with turquoise and silver jewelry, a concho belt around her tiny waist.

Maître d' Mario held out a chair for the woman; the big man positioned her next to it and said through teeth clenched around an aromatic pipe, "Your seat, darlin'." The Texan's accent was unmistakable. After she was seated, her husband pulled out the chair next to Samantha. "Ma'am, may I?" he asked, towering over her.

"Be my guest."

"Not everyday I get a chance to sit between two of the prettiest fillies this side of the Mississippi . . . hell, both sides." A flash of a smile was evident under his heavy white handlebar mustache, but the smile that lasted was in his twinkling eyes, set deep within the heavily wrinkled weathered skin under bushy brows. When seated he took off his Stetson and ran his fingers through thin white hair as he bent to place the hat under his chair.

"We're the Turners," Derek said, reaching across Samantha to shake the man's hand. "I'm Derek and my wife, Samantha." The man gave him a robust clasp. Derek suspected he wasn't the sick one.

"Judd Kramer. This here's my wife, Gracie."

"You're from Texas?" Derek asked.

"Hartley. A speck of a town in the Panhandle."

"What keeps you there?" Derek asked.

"The farm."

"Funny, I'd not thought of Texas as farmland. Ranching," Samantha said.

"Well, around Hartley it's farming land, all right. Maize." He took his wife's hand. "The little woman used to raise Arabian horses, but that was back in the good ol' days. Now we're just thankful to be reading the obit column every morning." The twinkle was back in his eye.

Derek looked behind the Texan to the three people following Mario. The taller of the two men wore a white linen jacket over a black T-shirt. His blue jeans had the look of newness, unlike his moccasins; and he carried his lean frame with noble bearing, taking long strides and yet stepping lightly. His features weren't conventionally handsome. His forehead was high, framed by a mane of steel-gray hair swept straight back and curled at the nape. He flicked the back of his hand along his neatly clipped salt-and-pepper whiskers. His generous aquiline nose and deep laugh lines gave his aging face character. He laid a hand on Gracie's shoulder, greeting her in a deep resounding voice as he took the chair next to her.

The couple behind him looked mismatched. They were about the same height, she being tall for a woman and he short for a man, about five-nine if Derek had to guess. She wore a tight black sleeveless, backless, and practically front-less leather dress that almost covered slim thighs at the top of long, long legs. Her shoulder-length hair was a tangled mass of curly locks of various colors. And like her roots, her eyes were brown, as were her brutally plucked eyebrows. Her lips, eyelids, and cheeks were colored in hues of magenta. She wore a spiked dog collar around her neck and right wrist. On her left arm were a dozen gold bracelets.

He was a handsome man, probably in his early fifties. He wore tortoise-rimmed glasses that matched all but the gray temples of his conservatively cut hair. Conservative, too, was his navy suit and red plaid tie.

Ignoring the chair Mario pulled out next to the taller man, the woman slipped into the seat next to Derek. The man in the navy suit gave an embarrassed smile and sat down beside her, leaving a seat empty between him and the taller newcomer.

"Cherry," the Texan said, "it's my pleasure to introduce the Turners, Samantha and Derek. Samantha, Derek, this lovely creature is Cherry; Warren Pruett has the honor of sitting next to her, and of course you know our celebrity, Billie Wade."

"I don't think so, Judd," Samantha said. "I'm sorry, Mr. Wade. I'm afraid your celebrity is wasted on me."

"Not really all that much of a celebrity. Had a little luck with my music."

Gracie laughed. "He's being modest. He's a very famous country and western musician."

"Now, Gracie," Billie said in his deep voice, "you shame me."

"Your wife isn't joining us for dinner, Mr. Wade?" Samantha asked.

"Billie, please." He picked up his water glass. "Cherry's my wife."

"Oh." Samantha nodded. "Your wife isn't joining us, Mr. Pruett?"

"Warren. No, she's not feeling up to dinner."

"I'd be happy to look in on her. I'm a doctor."

"No need, she's merely seasick. I'll take her some soup."

Samantha smiled. "I can identify with that. Our steward, Paul, said he's been seasick the whole two years he's worked cruises."

"Paul's your steward, too?" Cherry asked. "Doesn't he have the cutest set of buns? I just love him."

"Gee, I didn't notice. My vision's been blurry." Samantha turned to Derek, a sparkle in her dilated eyes. "Why didn't you tell me?"

"I don't need rivals."

"Gracie, I wish you could see him. He's just so cute. Like a teddy bear, so cute and cuddl—"

"Cherry," Billie said, "shut your stupid mouth."

Derek watched Gracie search for Billie's hand. She was blind. He hadn't noticed her unfocused eyes until now. "It's all right," Gracie said, patting Billie's hand.

The waiter, Favio, saved the day by sliding in next to Gracie. "Señora Kramer, so nice to have you at my table again. Could I interest you in an appetizer? Caviar, shrimp cocktail, or some fresh fruit with or without Triple Sec, or how about ham mousse soaked in sherry?"

"Fresh fruit would be nice."

"Soup? Capon broth with tortellini, cream of tomato, or beef bouillon?"

She absently fingered the squash blossom around her neck as she decided. "The broth with tortellini."

He finished writing and said, "Lobster tail with rice pilaf,

Red King Alaska salmon, spring chicken, or prime rib with Yorkshire pudding?"

"Better have the chicken."

"Creamy Italian on your salad?"

"Please."

"And then later I'll bring you your special dessert."

"No, that won't be necessary. Whatever everyone else is having."

Favio cocked an eyebrow, which was lost on the woman. "Now, Señora Kramer—"

Judd interrupted. "It's all right, Favio. Doc said she could have all the sweets she wants now."

Samantha pursed her lips. Derek would have to remember to ask her what she was thinking.

Later, as Cherry was dunking a forkful of lobster meat into her drawn butter, she said, "Look, there's Garth. How'd he rate getting a table for two?"

"Probably bribed the maître d' so he could have a little peace and quiet," Billie offered.

"Just as well." Cherry wiped a drop of butter off her chin. "His wife gives me the willies, twitching all the time. Looks more like his mother than his wife."

"Not true." Billie turned to Samantha. "She's a charming, articulate woman."

"Well, good thing she inherited her late husband's production company. That's all I can say." Cherry picked at her lobster. "Garth's a film producer."

"Quite a coincidence running into friends on the ship," Derek said.

"Oh, we didn't know them before. She was a patient at the Blanca Institute where Gracie and my husband were. They ate with us on the trip down."

Derek looked in the direction she had pointed when she first spotted Garth. She must have been talking about the dark-haired woman, a beauty in her day, for even now she was a handsome woman in her late sixties, early seventies. Although Derek saw only the man's tapered back, he gathered from the long ponytail that he was a good deal younger. "You mean the couple with a bottle of Cabernet Sauvignon on their table?"

"Let me see your glasses," Cherry said as she ripped Warren's glasses from his face. "Why do ya' bother to wear these, Warren?" She handed the glasses back. "I must be blinder than I thought. No offense, Gracie." To Derek, she added, "He's the one with the long hair. Is that who you meant?"

Derek nodded. That made four couples, not three. He'd have to remember to tell Woods that his informant was unreliable.

"Blanca Institute?" Samantha asked.

"Yeah, just left today." Cherry sighed. "Boring. Good thing Garth was there to take me around."

"What kind of institute—"

"Mrs. Turner," Warren called, "Favio is trying to . . . ah . . ."

Samantha looked over her shoulder. "Sorry," she said, moving out of his way.

"Where do you live, Cherry?" Derek asked while Samantha, Judd, Warren, and Gracie laughed at one of Billie's tour stories. Cherry had apparently heard them a million times and wasn't interested in listening to them again. She was more interested in watching Garth.

"Now we live in Nashville. We're going to be moving to LA. Going to get a beach house . . . maybe Malibu. Garth said I'd like Malibu."

Billie stopped in midsentence, folded his arms, and leaned across the table. "No, we're not. You're blowing smoke up your ass if you think I'm leaving Braxton Hill now that Susan and little Billy have come home."

Cherry's eyes narrowed until they were two smudged circles of magenta. She turned to Derek. "You'd think a thirty-year-old wouldn't need her daddy anymore."

Billie glared at her for a moment, and then straightened in his chair. "Sorry. Where was I? Oh, yes, the time Waylon and I made hobo chili on the Lake Tahoe shore."

Favio enticed them with a variety of desserts. He passed a soufflé laced with Grand Marnier under their noses, followed by a one-layered cake decorated in gold leaves. A silver tray of petits fours was set in the middle of the table.

He spooned out the soufflé to everyone but Billie, who announced he was watching his boyish physique, giving an extra helping to Samantha for the baby. The cake was divided, again with Samantha receiving an extra portion over her meek protests. Favio then moved the petits fours tray in front of Samantha for easy access. Gracie's portions, on the other hand, were very small. Favio knew she was not supposed to eat sugar, and mentioned it often.

After dinner, Samantha and Derek joined Cherry, Billie, and Garth in the Lido Lounge for a drink before the magic show. Billie had barely ordered tonic water with a twist of lime before he was persuaded to perform with the trio. He played the borrowed guitar while the pianist followed his lead. The drummer wandered in and out, but kept time with his foot.

Cherry tried her best to talk to Garth over the music, but Garth kept turning away to listen to Billie's guitar. He was older than he appeared across the dining room. Derek supposed he was closing in on fifty. He was tall and so thin it showed on his face. His intense gray eyes moved from one speaker to the next as if absorbing each morsel of thought. He spoke rapidly and used scholarly words that glided nimbly over his tongue.

"I'm sorry your wife wasn't up to this," Samantha said to Garth as Billie put down the guitar and started back to the table. He got as far as the first table, where he was now seated with five women.

"She's actually doing extremely well. Just needs some rest."

"Cherry was saying she was a patient in a clinic in St. Thomas."

Garth nodded.

"What was she being treated for?" Samantha asked.

Nice and subtle, my darling, Derek thought to himself.
"Parkinson's disease."

"Why come so far? Can't she get treatment in LA?"

He shrugged. "A friend recommended the Blanca Institute. Said they were leaps and bounds ahead of any treatment in the States. The FDA takes so long to approve
anything innovative. Red tape. Why should Vivian suffer
while inept bureaucrats drag their feet?"

"What are they doing for her? Treating her low dopamine
content in the basal ganglia with Levodopa and anticholin-
ergic agents?"

Cherry exploded in nervous laughter.

Garth pushed his drink back and wiped up the wet ring
with the cocktail napkin. "I don't actually know. She was
receiving injections of some sort."

"Did they say alcohol injections? Into the thalamus?"
Samantha pointed to her brain.

"Alcohol!" Cherry rattled the ice against the sides of her
empty glass. "Wouldn't that be a hoot? Giving Billie a shot
of alcohol in his liver!"

Samantha looked at her. "Billie was getting the same
treatment?"

"Sure. Water from the fountain of youth."

Garth shook his head. "I'm not certain what they were
getting. All I really know is that they were given a series of
four injections six hours apart. And I can't believe the
difference. She's a thousand times better. No tremors. It's a
miracle."

"Ditto for Billie. Though I liked him better when he was
sick," she added, almost under her breath.

"May I join you?" Warren asked. He had a drink in one
hand and a cigarette in the other.

"Certainly." Derek reached around and pulled up a chair
from the empty table behind them. Samantha's eyes were
riveted on him. The cigarette.

"Derek, I'm going to the rest room, then on in to get a
table for the magic show. Meet you there."

"I'll go with you," Garth said, fanning the air in front of him as he offered Samantha a hand.

"Me too," said Cherry, circling around to be on Garth's free side.

"Should you tell Billie where we're going?" Garth asked.

"He'll find us."

As the threesome left, Derek's eyes moved from Samantha's swollen ankles to Cherry's long legs and back again. "Do you have another cigarette?"

"Blows your surgical theory?" Derek asked as he placed Samantha's nightshirt on her bed.

"Apparently so." Samantha felt she looked worse than the Blanca Institute's patients. It was not a comforting thought. "Gracie can now tolerate sugar, she may have gotten islet cells from aborted fetal tissue. But what about the rest of them? Gracie was the only diabetic of the three. And Mrs. Pruett? Nothing adds up." She pulled her dress up above her hips and sat on the edge of the bed, sighing heavily. "The only explanation that makes sense is Cherry's about the fountain of youth."

"That's my cue to laugh?" He helped her out of her dress.

"There's nothing funny about it. A growing corps of molecular biologists, geneticists, immunologists, and other researchers are working to unlock the secrets of aging and illness. Tinkering with genes, diet, drugs. Why would it be so startling for life expectancy to be doubled or tripled? It's risen from 47.3 to 75.4 years in the United States since 1900. The Blanca Institute may have made significant strides toward intervention."

"Are we ready for an onslaught of hundred-and-fifty-year-olds? What would happen to the Social Security and heath-care systems? Young people not able to find jobs because the elderly have postponed retirement? Housing, food, and water?"

She crashed to the bed and stared up at the ceiling. "That's fifty years or so up the road. Couldn't we concern ourselves with the here and now?"

Derek took off his jacket and hung it up. He'd be happy if they didn't do even that.

"Maybe Garth's wife was injected with PBN—phenyl butyl nitrone—to combat the free radicals that run amok in Alzheimer's and Parkinson's."

"Free radicals?"

"Damaging oxygen byproducts that occur naturally in the body. They destroy fats and proteins that are crucial to the way cells function. There's some evidence to suggest that free radicals speed the aging process."

"This PBN. Has your father been injected with it?"

"No, only gerbils. It needs to win government approval to be tested in humans. I may be getting off the track. More likely they gave her an injection of alcohol in the thalamus. It is the acceptable treatment for paralysis agitans—Parkinson's disease. An alcohol injection would kill the offending cells that cause the hypokinetic or hyperkinetic features."

"Go over the last part again—in English."

"You know, the manifestations of tremors, the pill-rolling movement with the hands," she rolled her hand as if there were a little pill cupped in the palm, "like the sliding gait my father sometimes had when he walked."

Derek folded his pants over a hanger. "And Billie?"

"I would guess cirrhosis of the liver, from Cherry's remark about an alcohol injection. Livers don't rejuvenate. It wouldn't matter what they injected into Billie."

"What about a scam, Samantha? The fountain of youth is perfect. Give them a placebo injection to psyche them up, put them back on a luxury cruise ship, and send them on their merry way."

"What about the human tissue from the abortion clinics? Why involve them? And Doyle? He was murdered."

"He was going to expose their scam?"

"Who'd listen to him? Not anyone who was desperate enough to give it a try. There are so many unanswered questions. Maybe Gracie's already in a diabetic coma."

$\triangledown$

31

"WHICH ONE IS the CIA agent?" Sam whispered in Derek's ear as they climbed into the bus. "The bus driver or the guide?"

"Just yours truly."

Sam had her doubts. "Do you want the window seat?"

"Doesn't matter."

"Take it then. Just that much farther." She felt his hand glide across her bottom as he scooted in. "You sure this is the bus Vivian is riding on?"

"Should be. Though I don't see them. Wait . . . there they are. Looks like the whole crew except Mrs. Pruett."

Sam leaned over Derek to look out the window. Her vision still wasn't back to normal, but at least she had her very own sunglasses, which fit a great deal better than Derek's. "Gracie's going sightseeing? Well, so much for the diabetic coma theory."

"If we'd gotten up in time for breakfast, we'd already have known that."

"But I so enjoyed not getting up."

"Me, too." The unfailing lover lifted his sunglasses, giving her a good look at his eyes as he indicated something-or-other. She pretty well knew what he meant, but she pretended otherwise. "But if you were really a dedicated doctor you'd take your Hippocratic oath more seriously. And not be so concerned about your personal desires."

She sucked in a smile and traced her fingers up his leg. "I guess I'm just a hypocrite."

He plucked her hand and dropped it on her lap. "Don't toy with my emotions," he whispered. "Not unless you desire to be dragged off this bus and back to the stateroom."

It warranted a moment's thought, but hypocrisy can be carried just so far. Sam crossed and uncrossed her legs trying to get comfortable, an endless task. Their new friends greeted them as each filed past.

The bus lurched forward, signifying the beginning of Folly Number Two. She bent over and pulled at her tight khaki pants legs, relieving her sunburn pain not at all. The bus drove along the waterfront and then into town as the young mahogany-brown guide, with a French accent, pointed out this and that.

Crowded. White buildings crowded together to form the city. A matrix of whiteness dotted the lush green hillsides. Crowded, Sam soon discovered, because the town, or maybe the island, had a population of a hundred thousand. It also had had the same governor since 1955, a piece of trivia to impart to Kate. The churchyard was crowded with white shrines and eclectic statues over graves. Their first stop was just outside the town, a cathedral overlooking the Caribbean.

Sam slumped on the carved wooden pew in the back row next to Gracie while Derek and Judd bought French post-cards in an anteroom. She followed the gold trimming along the archway some three stories above the altar. Then she looked at the stained-glass windows, wondering what the scenes might have been.

"It's so impressive," Gracie said. "Listen to the echo. Feel the ray of light."

Gracie might have felt warmth from the light filtering through a nearby window, but it was the halo around Gracie's head that impressed Sam. She listened to the echo, but heard only Cherry giggling. She wasn't sure where it was coming from, but would bet Cherry wasn't with Billie. A safe bet would be Garth.

"They're loading the bus, ladies." Sam turned to see Garth standing behind them. Good thing she wasn't a betting person. "Your husbands are in line to buy postcards. Derek sent me to fetch you."

"Where's Cherry?"

"Ah," he looked around, "saw her with Warren a few minutes ago."

Warren. Sam had forgotten about him. As they were walking to the bus, Sam asked Gracie, "Do you mind if I ask you something about your stay in the institute?"

"No, not at all."

"Did they give you injections of islet cells into the pancreas?"

"How did you know that?"

"I read about it somewhere." Sam was truly impressed. This would revolutionize modern medicine. The current acceptable method was a piggyback transplant, with an extra pancreas being attached to the original dysfunctional one. "How did they get around the rejection problems? Did you have radiation and chemotherapy before coming down? Or were you at the clinic long enough to get it there?"

"Three days. They kept giving me pills from a little cup. And now I'm taking some twice a day."

"What do the pills look like? I'm sorry, Gracie. I wasn't thinking. Would you mind if I looked at them when we're back on board?" Would have been nice if Derek had packed her PDR.

She had so many questions. Why was Doyle killed? What was there to expose? It sounded like a Nobel Prize–winning achievement to her.

Sam threw her purse down on her seat and headed to the back of the bus where Billie was sitting. She interrupted his conversation with a couple of young women across the aisle. "Billie, could I speak with you a moment?"

He slid over and patted the seat beside him.

Sam sat, a little less gracefully than she would have liked. "My father has Alzheimer's and I'm wondering if maybe he could benefit from a trip to the Blanca Institute."

He shook his head. "I don't know. It worked for me."

"Do you mind if I ask what part of your body received the injection?"

"My stupid liver."

"Do you know what the injection was?"

"A tissue builder of some sort."

At least he didn't say water from the fountain of youth. "It's supposed to rejuvenate your liver?"

"That, and not drinking."

Not drinking was probably the real secret. "I'll talk to you later. I see my husband."

He put his hand on the swell at her middle. He did it so naturally she couldn't take offense. "When are you due?"

"Eight weeks."

"Not long."

"It depends on your perspective. From where I'm sitting, it's a long time."

"Making time with the celebrity, I see," Derek said as she sat down next to him.

"Did you get some postcards or were you merely talking to a cohort?"

Derek leaned over the seat and took a brown sack out of a side pocket of his camera case. "Genuine French postcards, wrapped in plain brown paper. I'll show them to you in the privacy of our room."

"Which only makes me want to see them now!" She whipped them out of his hand.

"The writing's in French. That's a picture of the cathedral, the next—" he waited until she was staring at it—"is a picture of Mount Pelee. Then several of the island."

She handed them back. "Risqué."

"Gee, now you've spoiled tonight's games."

She gave him her best smile. "You're such a tease. All talk, no action."

"I beg your pardon."

"Beg all you like."

Derek patted her knee. "How are you feeling?"

"Well, I have a headache, a backache, sick to my stomach,

my vision's still not in focus, my toes and feet itch, my sunburn hurts like hell—excuse me, hurts rather severely—the baby's defying nature by doing flips and still keeping an angry foot against my ribs, the ground keeps swaying, and I wish I'd gone to the bathroom."

"That's a relief. I was afraid your lips might be bruised." He kissed her.

"But I'm feeling much better."

Cherry sashayed past. "Is that the biggest Jesus you ever did see or what?" Cherry was talking about the statue in front of the steeple.

Warren, directly behind her, replied, "You've never been to Rio, I take it."

Their next stop was near a little waterfall well into the jungle. The bus had maneuvered around a caravan of military jeeps and transports along the two-lane road. Black soldiers relaxed on big boulders along the banks and in the lazy river, about as wide but much deeper than the one flowing through the ranch. Under a clump of trees near the river stood four black men dressed in blue shirts and black pants, each with a machete in hand. Sam took them for the island's park maintenance men. Derek and Warren were hiding behind one of the three buses, sneaking a smoke. The two men were spending a great deal of time together; she was beginning to wonder if maybe there was more to their cigarette breaks than met the eye. Maybe there was no Mrs. Pruett.

As she stood admiring the outhouse at the other end of the long line of mostly women, a black cat came out of nowhere to rub up against her swollen legs.

"Wonder what kind of tropical diseases she's carrying?" Vivian, who had gotten in line behind her, asked in a husky voice.

Sam stepped away from the cat and turned to face Vivian and Garth. "That would be bad luck, wouldn't it?" The cat rubbed all the harder against her legs. "Persistent, isn't she?"

Garth nudged it away with his foot.

"This is absolutely my favorite island." Vivian took in a deep breath of the sickeningly sweet-scented jungle air. "We were here on location in the fifties to shoot *The Day the World Ended.*"

"Did you see it?" Garth asked Sam as he wiped clumps of cat hair off the sides of his pants. "Vivian was nominated for an Oscar."

"I lost."

"You should have won."

So, Billie wasn't the only celebrity in the group, though unlike male actors, who only get better with age, too many actresses slip into obscurity. And now she didn't even have her health, though as far as Sam could see, Vivian manifested no signs of Parkinson's. But she still held fast to her conviction that the woman was treated with an injection of alcohol. "What was it about?"

"The 1902 eruption of Mount Pelee. Should be able to see the volcano in a few miles."

After her turn at the outhouse Sam climbed on a bus. Then she climbed off and crossed the road to her bus. She noticed Derek watching. Nothing missed his eagle eyes.

Soon Derek was pointing out cloud-covered Mount Pelee as it appeared at a distance above the coffee trees that lined this section of the road. Sam looked briefly and then turned away. "It makes me sick to my stomach to look out the window."

He laced his fingers with hers and then kissed the back of her hand. It was her reward for whining.

No sooner did they emerge from the jungle than they were riding along the sandy beach of the blue sea. Moments later St. Pierre loomed ahead.

"They all died unnecessarily," Vivian said in her throaty voice as she and Sam crossed the narrow street just ahead of Garth and Derek. "Thirty thousand people died that morning when Mount Pelee blew its top. It might as well have been an atomic explosion. There were only two survivors, a prisoner in an underground cell and a madman. Why the madman survived no one seems to know."

The town was a shell now, a few blocks long. A picture in the museum taken several weeks after the destruction showed a thick cloud of superheated gas covering St. Pierre and rising hundreds of feet into the air. Time hadn't altered the sense of disaster, and it left Sam with the same hollow feeling as the plane crash. But this was a natural disaster, in Sam's mind and soul, more acceptable. Nor had she been responsible for the deaths here.

"Over here, Samantha," Vivian called. "Look at the picture of the theater. I'll show you the ruins after we leave here."

They took a quick look at the murky pictures and rancid artifacts. A disproportionate number of crucifixes survived. An enormous metal bell, crushed in on one side, occupied the middle floor space.

The theater ruins consisted of stone steps and a dirt lot with two crumbling walls at the perimeters. Everything was the color of gray ash.

"The jail's right down the street," Vivian said. "Shall we walk down to it?"

Derek grasped hold of Sam's shoulders just as she heard the whumping of a descending helicopter. Something about his silence alarmed her. "What does it mean, Derek?"

"It means not all tourists came by bus." To Vivian, he added, "We're running out of time, we'd better skip the jail."

The helicopter landed on the beach across from the bus, out of their sight.

They got as far as St. Pierre's equivalent of a Seven-Eleven. The front room was bare save for a Pepsi clock on the wall, its black hands dangling straight down as if too tired to do anything but let gravity have its way, a black wrought-iron postcard rack, a stool in the corner where the elderly storekeeper was perched, and an old commercial freezer containing a limited variety of ice cream bars.

Sam asked directions to the rest room. The woman got up, shuffled to the even barer back room, and opened an antique refrigerator. Proudly she displayed a supply of Coke bottles and offered Sam her choice. "No, I wanted a rest room."

The stooped woman chose one for her. Sam seized it by its sweaty neck. "Derek," she shouted.

Mr. Faithful Interpreter peeked around the corner.

"Would you ask her where the rest room is?"

The two exchanged words. The woman slapped her open palm against the side of her temple, and led Sam out the back door.

When Sam got back she found a group of strangers in the store. Another bus. Derek was gone. Woods's words about the last train came to mind and she hurried to the bus.

On the street she found Derek in an uncharacteristically heated argument with a stranger in a suit. They stopped when she approached. "Derek?"

"Did you pay for that?" He pointed to the Coke in her hand.

"Didn't you?"

"No," he reached into his pocket and pulled out a few folded bills, "go back and pay for it."

Sam started back, then turned. They were staring at her. She waited in line with the strangers, feeling an unnamed anxiety, and when it was finally her turn handed the woman all of the money. The old woman looked through the bills with disgust, peeled off the top, and rummaged through her cigar box. It took most of what she had to make change.

Derek and the stranger stopped when she was within earshot. "Give me a minute," Derek said to him.

The man backed away and Derek led her toward the bus. "I have to go with him."

"What?" Sam glanced back at the man, seeing her reflection in his sunglasses. "Who is he? Where are you going? Something about the clinic?"

"It doesn't have anything to do with the clinic, that I can tell you. I'll be back as soon as I can. If I'm not back by the time you dock in Florida—"

"Florida! Where are you going?"

He embraced her, burying her face in his chest until she couldn't breath, let alone talk. "Calm down." She struggled to free herself but he was stronger and more determined to keep her there. "I have a fairly good rapport with a group of people who want to do something our government doesn't want them to do, at least not for the time being. They want me to talk to them. I'll catch up with you as soon as I can." He cupped her chin and raised her head. "I'm sorry."

A helpless feeling drove through her, but she couldn't think of anything to say to make him stay. "Will you be safe?"

"Of course." He seemed insulted, as if she had questioned his abilities. "I'll have someone come to keep you company."

So much for her notion that Warren was a cohort. "I have plenty of company."

"You know what I mean. And don't throw whoever comes over the rail," he added with a smile.

In the end, she raised up and kissed him.

"I have to go," he said. He took her arm and led her a few more steps to where Judd, pipe clenched between teeth, Warren, flicking ashes to the ground in boredom, and Billie, hands in his Levi's back pockets, were male-bonding. "Would you men take care of my wife until I get back?" Derek pointed to the helicopter. "No rest for the wicked."

Sam vaguely felt his lips brush across her forehead. "I love you." She nodded slowly as he raced away, never turning to look back.

"Happy Thanksgiving, Derek."

32

"HAPPY THANKSGIVING," everyone said in unison as they raised their goblets. Sam touched her water goblet to Judd's wine goblet, and then turned and reached across Derek's empty chair to get at Cherry's. Cherry really put herself out to click glasses with her.

"A darn shame about Derek." Judd downed his wine.

"It was just like something out of the movies," Cherry added excitedly, "running over the sandy beach toward the helicopter, ducking under the whirling blades, lifting up and circling over the water, and then disappearing. Bet Garth uses it in his next movie."

Sam stared at the girl a bit too long, dazzled by the purple-sequined dress that plunged to her waist. Sam almost hoped Derek would miss the rest of the cruise. Somehow she suspected Cherry would be latching onto him. Derek's wasn't the only empty seat at the table. Mrs. Pruett was still in her cabin.

"Warren, has your wife seen the ship's doctor?"

"Oh, yes. She's fine as long as she's lying down."

"I take it her treatment at the Blanca Institute proscribes a motion-sickness injection."

Cherry fawned all over Warren. "I didn't know you guys were at the clinic. Did you, Judd?"

"Sorry, Warren, if we'd known we'd have made you feel welcome."

Sam looked over at Billie, who was staring at Warren. She couldn't read his mind, but suspected he was wondering how

Cherry could have missed Warren at the clinic. Sam had to admit it crossed her mind.

She ate the turkey dinner as if it were plastic, her mind on Derek. Where was he? What had been so important? She hadn't seen hide nor hair of the bodyguard, yet. Not that he would give her news of Derek.

When the table was being cleared for pumpkin pie and a flaming dessert, Sam excused herself. She took the elevator to the floor she thought the purser's office was on only to find that she was on the balcony above it. She walked along the snapshot-lined gallery, not bothering to look for Derek's and hers. At the circular stairs she discovered a family at the bottom posing for the photographer. She tried to wait them out but gave up when she heard the mother say, "Take one of just the children."

She turned around and headed out to the elevators. Diners were everywhere now and the elevator was packed. She started down the main stairs against the flow.

"Coming up to the Carousel Lounge, Mrs. Turner?"

She looked across the crowd to see Warren. "Still haven't gotten to the purser's office. Thought it was on the Aloha Deck."

"Fiesta Deck, next one down."

Sam smiled her thanks. She wished the guys hadn't taken Derek so literally about watching after her.

The purser's office was jammed, and Sam cursed the photographer under her breath as she got into line, and then got out of line when she saw *Satellite World News* on the corner of the counter. She picked up a copy and hurried out. Looking at the fuzzy print, she sat down at the first of a long line of card tables and rummaged through her bag, her eyes scanning the larger and bolder blue-printed headlines: LATIN DICTATOR TOPPLED IN COUP. Her heart skipped a beat.

She put on her glasses and read. "The report could not be immediately confirmed. It followed several hours of heavy gunfire in the streets. There was no confirmation of casualties, but eyewitnesses told the Associated Press there were hundreds of dead and wounded." Her hand was shaking so badly that she had to lay the paper down on the table to finish the article. She was jumping to conclusions. Derek might not have been there.

Somehow she managed to get back to Aloha Deck and her cabin.

"Is something the matter, Mrs. Turner?"

"I can't find my key, Paul."

The steward snaked his hand under his gray uniform shirt for a fat ring of keys. "May I get you something? Tea? Soup?" he asked as he pushed the door back.

"Soup."

"And some tea?"

She shook her head. "No, not for me. Mrs. Pruett. He forgot her soup." Warren was empty-handed when she'd passed him on the stairs. "Mr. Pruett forgot to get her soup. Did you get her some?"

He pointed behind him to stateroom 809 and the Do Not Disturb sign on the door. "No."

She'd find Warren.

The performance had started by the time she reached the Carousel Lounge. Sam looked along the six or so horseshoe rows of seats, but couldn't see Warren.

"We saved you a seat," Judd said, appearing from out of thin air and taking her arm.

"Is Warren with you?" she asked as they negotiated the stairs.

"Sure as shootin'."

The performers were spilling over into the aisles. Sam practically sat on someone's lap to get out of a dancer's way. Garth scooted over for Sam before beckoning the cocktail waitress.

"What's your pleasure, Samantha?"

"A glass of water."

"Bring us another round," Garth said to the petite Asian girl, "and a glass of water."

Warren's attention was on the dancers decked out in buccaneer and damsel-in-distress costumes. About the time the women clutched at their shredded bodices and the men began fencing, she called out to Warren. "You forgot your wife's soup."

"Paul got it for her tonight." He turned back to the dancers.

Why was Warren lying?

$\triangledown$

33

"Ah, a 49ers fan."

Sam wiped sleep from her eyes with the hand not holding the door open. "What do you want, Billie?"

"I come bearing the innards of the Cornucopia and you ask me what I want." Billie brushed past her.

"But, ah . . ."

He set a breakfast tray on Derek's unslept bed. "Derek told us to take care of you. I don't take my charges lightly."

She'd been awake most of the night worrying about Derek and Mrs. Pruett. She really didn't need an early-morning caller. "I, ah . . ." Sam pointed to the bathroom.

"Hurry up if you must, but don't let your coffee get cold."

She hurried and was back to find he hadn't left. "You really shouldn't have bothered." She sat on the foot of her bed, pulling the nightshirt over her knees. "I don't always eat breakfast."

"You should. It's the most important meal of the day. Especially now," he added, handing over a Styrofoam cup of coffee.

"Thanks."

"Sugar, cream." He held up little packets.

She shook her head and sipped the lukewarm coffee.

"I didn't know what you'd like so I brought . . . fruit—" he held up a white Styrofoam bowl—"and a plate of sweet rolls."

Sam held up the coffee when he tried to hand over the fruit.

"Don't have all day. We're going shopping as soon as you get dressed."

Sam wasn't going shopping, or anyplace else. She had her own agenda for the day. She placed the cup on the vanity and then pointed to the fruit. He handed it over faster than a hungry man could skin a rabbit. "I thought I'd just stay on board today."

"And mope?"

"Did you bring a napkin?"

He held up a batch, and then spread one across her lap. "You can always tell a mother in a self-service restaurant. She's the one pulling napkin after napkin out of the dispenser."

"Apparently not only mothers do it, I see."

"Ah, but I used to be a mother. It's a habit you don't break."

"You're not telling me you used to be a woman?"

He laughed. "Just a mother. After my first wife ran off."

"I'm sorry."

Billie shrugged. "It's been a long time. She's dead now, anyway. Overdose."

"I'm sorry."

"It was hard on the kids." Billie, the mother, pushed the plate of rolls as close to her as he could manage without dumping them into her lap. "She was the only woman I ever really loved."

Sam wondered how often he mentioned it to Cherry. "Hurts to lose someone you love. My first husband died suddenly of a coronary. I'm still not over it and it's been seven years." Why were they telling each other these things?

"Heart attack. Don't usually think of a young person going that way."

Explaining the difference between coronary and heart attack seemed unimportant. "John was in his mid-fifties at the time. A May-December marriage like yours." Sam noticed a faraway look in his eyes. "He was Derek's father." She nibbled on a blueberry muffin. "I don't usually tell people that. Guess maybe I'm telling you because . . . I'd like us to be close enough to talk about something else. I hate to see Cherry and you so unhappy. Maybe you can patch things up."

Sparks flew as he shook his mane. "She's not the woman I married." Memory curled his lips. "She was the best damned waitress I'd ever seen. A little greasy spoon in Elko, Nevada. Could hardly take a sip of coffee before she'd refill it. Didn't even know who I was. Missed my concert in Reno hanging around Elko trying to get her to run off with me."

Sam threw down a bran muffin. She'd polished off the blueberry and had been working her way through the rest of the rolls. Strolling down memory lane with Billie wasn't the best way to burn off calories. "What went wrong?"

"We wanted different things. She wanted to live in the fast lane. I wanted the slow, easy pace down home. And I wanted her to be waiting for me when I'd get home after being on the road."

The chocolate croissant was beyond belief! "Here, take this away." She thrust breakfast back at him. "You and Cherry don't have children?"

"She wouldn't be a fit mother. Look at her. She's bad enough around my grandson. Always griping."

"Maybe she's jealous. Maybe she wants a child of her own."

"Yeah, that must have been why she had an abortion last spring."

She was sure striking out in the theory department of late. "And then on the other hand, maybe I don't know what I'm talking about."

Billie leaped beside her and put an easy hand on her abdomen. "Children are a big responsibility. You owe them, and if you can't deliver, it's best not to bring them into the cold, cruel world."

It wasn't her place to condemn abortions. She could never have one herself, but who was she to tell someone what they could or couldn't do? She decided to keep her opinion to herself. "Here," she took his leathered hand—he hadn't always lived the life of a famous musician—and placed it just under her rib cage, "can you feel the little foot? He just loves to kick me in the ribs."

Billie grinned like a little boy who'd just hit a home run. "It kicked my hand."

"It says St. Maarten is divided between two sovereign powers, the French and the Dutch. This is the Dutch side."

"Look," Cherry said, pointing up the narrow, shop-lined street, "there's Gucci."

"Well, go," Billie said, shooing her ahead. "I'll be there in plenty of time to pay the bill."

Garth continued to read to Sam out of the guide book. Vivian was spending the better part of the day in the ship's beauty spa. "English is widely spoken. On the Dutch side, you'll hear Papiamento, a patois combining elements of Spanish, Dutch, English, and some African and Indian words that originated in Aruba and Curaçao."

Derek probably spoke Papiamento fluently. She hoped he was safe.

"Currency . . . Dollars are accepted everywhere, so there's no need to change money."

"As is plastic," Billie added dryly.

Sam fell behind a pace looking for Warren. She'd made up her mind to call on his wife as soon as she could free herself of her caretakers; Billie had refused to let her stay aboard and she wasn't up to fighting about it.

"Cherry had better hope Gucci has come out with new goods. She has everything else," Billie said as they walked into the store.

Sam sat on the white cane settee as Garth tried on shoes and Billie fingered the wallets. Cherry was downstairs looking at luggage, someone said.

Garth stuck his head around the potted palm tree. "Are you going to buy anything?"

Sam shrugged. "Guess maybe if something jumps out at me."

"A watch?"

She held up her Timex. "Have one."

"I wonder if Derek knows how lucky he is," Garth muttered as he wandered off.

The bell over the door tinkled as Warren wandered in.

"Tired?"

She nodded.

"The edema's gone down."

Sam hoisted the white sundress and straightened out her legs. "I can't see it."

He knelt down and grasped her heel. He pressed his thumb into the skin against the subcutaneous aspect of the tibia. He withdrew his thumb and noted the depth of the pit. The edema had gone down. "The burn looks better today."

Sam didn't get it. He seemed nice enough, but why did he say that about the soup? If his wife had been asleep or something and didn't want the soup, why didn't he say so? "Feels better. And my vision's no longer blurry."

He got to his feet and pushed his glasses up. "I'm going up the street. See you later."

The bell tinkled as he left. He was an odd one.

"This is for the baby." Billie handed Sam a large gift-wrapped box.

"What is it?" she asked as she ran her fingertips over the slick paper.

"A diaper bag. Open it."

"No, it's too pretty to open. I want Derek to see it."

"What if you don't like it or it's the wrong style?"

"I'll love it. It's the thought that counts, and we'll treasure it."

Billie sat down beside her. "Wish I'd met you first."

She squeezed his coarse hand. It was mildly leathered to the wrist like she'd seen so often on old ranchers around Sheridan. Cherry breezed by behind an Asian salesgirl. They had made the trip upstairs to check out a suitcase in the window. Cherry wore tight white short shorts and a baby blue sleeveless knit top that showed off her nipples quite nicely. After the two made the trek back down the stairs, Sam said, "Billie, I know it's none of my business and feel free to tell me to shut up, but I've been thinking about Cherry's abortion. Maybe she was just cutting off her nose to spite her face." Woods had inspired her. "I mean, maybe she did it to get back at you."

"Get back at me for what?"

She shrugged. "I don't know. Not paying enough attention to her, telling her your first wife was the only woman you ever loved, something like that." He bent his head and leaned forward, his hands between his knees. She may have hit upon his transgression. "Seems you're always arguing. Maybe she acts so outrageously to make you angry . . . or to get your attention?"

The silence was most uncomfortable. She would have made a rotten psychiatrist.

"Samantha?" Garth pulled a small package out of a big Gucci shopping bag.

"Another one?"

"It's the wallet that matches the purse Billie bought."

Sam caught Billie's eye. "He said it was a diaper bag."

"That's what I meant. This is a diaper pin bag."

"You guys! You're making me feel—"

"Your stomach moved," Garth said in disbelief.

Her midsection held their undivided attention. Sam smoothed out the dress so they could see better if the baby did another flip-flop. "Do you want to put your hand on it?"

Garth stepped back like a frightened child.

"Come on." She reached out, taking his hand and placing it over the last site the baby kicked, then quickly slid it to the next flick. "Feel it?"

Garth's eyes grew wide. "I thought your stomach would be soft." So now they knew he didn't have kids.

"What in the world are you guys doing?" Cherry asked as she lumbered forth, burdened with packages.

"Come feel the baby move, Cherry," Billie said.

"It's hard," Garth added.

She dumped the packages in front of Billie and headed toward the door. "Come on, we have to hurry."

"If you don't believe in miracles all you have to do is look at babies. One itsy-bitsy egg that grows until it blossoms into a human being." Billie started gathering up packages. "You know the first thing I did when my children were born? I unwrapped the blanket and counted toes to make sure they had ten."

"This one has ten feet. The RNA coding—Shit! Embryologic precursors!"

Billie dropped the packages and dragged her back to the settee. "No, Samantha, it may feel like ten feet, but I know you'll have a healthy baby. You're feeling elbows, and arms, and knees. That's all it is."

She didn't want to sit down. She had to think. "The tissue building they injected into your liver had to be embryologic precursors. The cells wouldn't know any better than to rebuild the organ. A fertilized ovum divides for the first seventy-two hours as precursors before undergoing RNA processing. It would be like an orphaned kitten being taken in by a nursing bitch. It couldn't help but think it's a puppy."

"Okay."

"And precursors filled in the lesions in Vivian's basal ganglia."

Garth started to say something but Sam was in before him.

"That's where the abortion clinics come in. No." She stopped pacing and sat down in defeat. The aborted fetus would be well beyond the precursor stage. "Even if you could get the bitch to not reject the kitten, you wouldn't stick him back on a tourist ship with an impaired immune system."

Billie put a hand on her forehead. "She doesn't feel feverish."

"Feverish!" She knocked away his hand. "I'm fine except for a little edema."

"Edema?"

Wait a minute. Warren called it edema and knew how to check for pitting. "The medically correct term for excessive accumulation of interstitial fluid is edema." She held up her feet. "My swollen ankles. Did either of you know that?"

They didn't. But from their blank stares she feared they thought the swelling had gone to her brain.

Cherry was back. "Billie!"

Billie looked at each of them as if he couldn't decide what he should do.

"Billie, are you coming or not?"

Both men thought she was off her rocker. So what if Warren knows how to measure edema. Maybe he was a medic in the Army. Maybe his wife has swollen ankles. She was going to find out. "Go on, Billie, I'm fine. I'm going back to the ship."

"I'll go with her," Garth assured him.

$\triangledown$

34

A DUO WAS playing a Bob Dylan song as Garth and Sam walked through the Lido Lounge on the way to the stairs. She sat down. "I need to catch my breath. Why don't you leave me here? You don't have to bother to see me to my cabin."

"No bother."

She wanted to shake him; she needed to see Warren's wife before he got back from town. If only she had Doyle Smith's letter. What was he going to tell the authorities? It was something so terrible that someone was willing to kill to keep it secret.

"Would you like something to drink Samantha? Or how about lunch?"

"No lunch. Billie made me shovel it down at breakfast. Water would be nice."

Garth summoned the cocktail waitress. It was sweet of him to ask her to put in a twist of lime, but it would be more thoughtful to leave her alone. "Garth, what was it like at the institute?"

"Pleasant. Vivian's room was more a hotel suite than a hospital room." He sighed. "What's going on?"

"What do you mean?"

"Is the Blanca Institute under investigation? Is that it?"

How was she going to answer Garth's question? She twisted around to clap for the musicians. The keyboard player thanked the half-dozen appreciative listeners and announced the next tune. She'd stalled about as long as she could. She turned back. "My father has Alzheimer's disease. I'd like to believe there's a cure for him at the Blanca Institute. My medical training makes me skeptical. The fountain of youth is only a myth."

"Vivian is cured. If you only could have seen her before." Garth fell silent as the drinks were served. "Billie was a pathetic sight. Gracie's improvement isn't as dramatic but, believe me, Billie and Vivian are new people. I don't care if they're using apricot pits or water from the fountain of youth. Whatever it was, it cured Vivian and that's all that matters."

No, that's not all that matters. She knew of fifty people who may have lost their lives over whatever-it-is. She thought of the two little boys, the housewife who left a husband and three children, the straight-A college student whose mother had come from West Virginia to claim the remains. Sam had sat so patiently while the woman told her story of how the recruiting scout from Sheridan College had come to their small town, tucked away in the Appalachians, to watch her daughter play basketball, and how he had offered her a full scholarship that very evening. "What about Warren's wife?"

He shook his head. "I don't think it worked for her."

"Why do you say that?"

"They didn't come back in the limo with us. They brought her by ambulance."

"Did you see her at the institute?"

"No, but I passed her in the hall when Warren was wheeling her to their stateroom."

Warren said she was merely seasick. But then it wasn't his first lie. "Did she manifest any signs of her illness?"

Garth shrugged "Nothing that I noticed. She was pale."

Sam gulped down her water. "I'm going to my stateroom to lie down. Finish your drink." She had picked up her Gucci sack so Garth wouldn't have an excuse to find her and was gone before he had a chance to do anything about it.

Paul wasn't hard to find; he was putting clean towels in

the room across from hers. "Paul, I told Mr. Pruett I'd check in on his wife. Would you open the door for me, please?"

He took some towels and a couple of bars of soap from his cart. "Good, will give me a chance to straighten up." Sam followed him down the hall. He nodded to the Do Not Disturb sign on the door. "It makes it so terribly difficult for me."

Sam unburdened him of his towels as he opened the door. She brushed past him but faltered as the sunlight pouring through the porthole highlighted the red hair on the pillow. She stole closer.

Tiffany and she were in a close race to see who could go to seed faster. Tiffany had localized swelling of the eyelids and lips. Her hair was greasy but she and her expensive moisturizers had been separated for some time if Sam could go by the dry skin that made her face look like crackled paint on an antique porcelain doll. She needed more than a few strokes of her eyebrow pencil to cover her naked brows.

Paul took the towels from her. "Is she asleep?"

"Drugged." Sam folded down the covers to her chest. Her respiration was depressed. "Tiffany, can you hear me?"

Sam lifted the eyelids.

The evidence suggested that Warren's sedative of choice was phenobarbital, a Schedule IV drug. The Bureau of Narcotics and Dangerous Drugs kept a tight reign on things like that. Warren was either in a position to steal it, or, in light of the impressive edema physical, Warren was a doctor and, like Sam, had his very own BNDD number.

Warren would not have looked out of place at Dr. Sommers's lecture, though she couldn't swear that he was one of the two men who walked out moments before Doyle collapsed. Not that he had to leave. Simple enough to melt into the crowd during the confusion. She bet he owned a gray suit and a black Lexus. But what of Alan Martin Number Two? Were they in cahoots? Did Warren pay Alan to kill Doyle, then kill Alan to cover?

"I need to call my husband's office in the States. How should I go about it?"

Paul looked over her shoulder to Tiffany. "Is Mrs. Pruett going to die?"

Sam gave him a reassuring smile. "No, she's not going to die, but she isn't Mrs. Pruett. She's Tiffany Smith. Warren Pruett has kidnapped her."

"Kidnapped! Mr. Pruett?"

Sam squeezed his arm. "How about the phone? I have to call the CIA."

"Your husband's office? The CIA?"

She nodded. "The phone."

"Go to the communications room." He turned to point out directions, but instead doubled over and fell across the foot of the bed, pinning Tiffany's lower extremities. Towels flew. The top towel was bloodstained.

Warren came into the room and clicked the door closed behind him. The gun he pointed was elongated. A silencer, she'd wager.

She waited long enough to get comfortable with the notion that he wasn't going to shoot again, and then squatted down and felt Paul's carotid artery.

"Samantha, no heroics. I don't want to have to shoot him again."

"No need," she said as she pulled away. There was a faint pulse, but he probably wouldn't make it unless that bodyguard of Derek's showed up this very moment and saved the day. She sat down on the floor as her legs gave way. An adrenaline surge was the only thing keeping her going.

Warren didn't take her word for it. He checked for a pulse. He gave a noncommittal shrug.

"He's turning blue, he isn't breathing." The color of death is blue when breathing stops first, gray if the heart goes first. "And while I'm at it, Tiffany's having an allergic reaction to the phenobarbital you gave her."

"Secobarbital." He gave Tiffany a perfunctory glance.

"The swelling in her eyelids and lips," she pointed out.

He wasn't impressed. "It won't kill her."

Yeah, but would he? "Why did you kill Paul?"

He flipped the corpse over and onto the floor. Sam scooted out of the way in the nick of time. "I didn't, you did." Her carotid artery must have been at a runaway. He was going to kill her and make it look like a murder-suicide. "I couldn't let him live after you told him who she was. Derek's with the CIA? How much does he know? Where is he?"

It took her a moment to catch on. Keeping her big mouth shut seemed healthier. And stalling for time seemed a good idea, as well. She'd left the Gucci bag at her door—maybe Garth would see it and come looking for her. To what end? Paul's?

"Answer me!"

Tiffany and she both cried out, though Tiffany's cry sounded more like pain than fear. Warren noticed, too. He threw back Tiffany's covers and pulled up her nightgown. Sam didn't have the greatest vantage point but she could see a stained dressing. He started to put the gun down to look at the wound, but thought better of it.

"Here," he wheeled the gun at her, "look at the sutures."

Sam got to her feet. He had no idea what it cost her. In spite of the tremor in her hand, she pulled up the blood-soaked surgical tape on the near side, exposing a transverse midline incision. There was moderate seepage, but the sutures were intact. What had he done to her? Why was she on the ship? So many questions and hardly any answers. "They're fine," she told him in a thin voice. She moved her head out of the way for his inspection.

"He's a butcher."

"You didn't do this?"

"Of course not. An oophorectomy was entirely uncalled for. Pounce Blanca is a researcher, not a clinician."

An oophorectomy, excision of the ovaries. Now it all made sense. She was right about the embryologic precursors. They were farming them. Fertilize the eggs, let them divide for a couple of days, and inject the cells into their patients.

She had to agree with Warren. An oophorectomy to extract eggs was barbaric. Egg donations, common now that postmenopausal pregnancies were the rage, could be accomplished with a suction tube.

Warren threw a new dressing and an alcohol prep pad at her. A roll of surgical tape sailed by. Scissors were not forthcoming. She ripped open the dressing and alcohol with ease, but her teeth proved no match for the sturdy tape. "Would scissors be too much to ask?"

He nodded and laid out a dress.

"We're going somewhere?" she asked between gnaws.

Warren didn't answer.

Tiffany was coming around by the time they had her dressed, though she exhibited signs of drowsiness, lethargy, and, worst of all, vertigo. Getting the comb through Tiffany's hair would have been a great deal simpler if she didn't keep falling back onto her pillow. Warren could have been a sight more helpful. It wasn't like Sam was a nurse or a mortician and went about doing such chores every day of her life.

"Why did you have to kill everyone on the plane?"

"I had no choice. Tiffany thought you had the letter." His laugh frightened her. "She found it in his airline ticket jacket the day after the funeral."

The airline ticket! She had had it in her hand when she opened the safe. What about the dozen funerals they had in Sheridan? Didn't life mean anything to him? "What was in that damned letter, anyway?" He didn't answer, but she pretty well knew what it said. "Guess the authorities would close the Blanca Institute and the clinics in LA and Denver fast enough if they knew you were farming embryologic precursors."

He shrugged. "We'd certainly have enough do-gooders on our backs, but I don't think they'd have cause to close the institute."

What was she missing? What insidious thing was she missing?

"Now, we need to move the corpse to your room and take the wheelchair out of the storage room."

Their cleanup chores done and Tiffany secured in the

wheelchair, Sam asked again, "What was in the letter?"

"Take out your stateroom card. And don't force me to hurt anyone else." Warren stuck his gun under his belt buckle and replaced it with a nasty-looking knife.

"I hope you shoot your dick off."

He looked at her disapprovingly as he moved the gun to his hip. "You may push the wheelchair."

The Officer of the Day reminded them that the ship sailed at six. Somehow Sam suspected it would be sailing without them.

35

"IT'S A GODDAMN pirate ship!" Sam shouted as Warren gave her a hand with the wheelchair up the gangplank. "I'm being kidnapped aboard a goddamn pirate ship!"

"I can assure you your husband and his crew won't be pouring over the sides with swords drawn."

"Of all these sailboats why did you charter a pirate ship?"

"Because the captain and his wife, and the mate, speak only French. Lucky you made such a big deal over not speaking French."

"Lucky for you, maybe." He'd latched onto that a great deal sooner than she had about Warren's glasses when Cherry borrowed them to see what kind of wine Garth and Vivian were drinking. She should have known then that they were a disguise to keep them from recognizing him as the Lexus man at the airport. Why hadn't Derek realized? That's the kind of thing you'd think a spy would spot.

"Remember what I told you."

She could forget that he threatened to kill the French people if she caused any trouble? He said something to one of the men, a slender dark-haired man of about thirty. The man directed his words to Sam. Sam smiled and for no special reason said, "Thank you."

A fiftyish woman came out of the galley with a cup in hand. Her deeply tanned skin looked like Billie's leathered hands. She said something to which Warren said something. Sam made up her mind right then and there that if Derek did vault over the side of the ship with sword in hand to rescue his damsel in distress, she was going to learn French, and Spanish, and even Papiamento.

"She asks if you want anything to drink."

"Hemlock. I'll share."

He smiled, though on him it looked more like a sneer. He shook his head and said something. Sam took it that she wasn't going to get a drink. Tiffany wasn't having any either; she was zonked out again.

Sam dropped to a shellacked deep brown wooden bench under the low canvas shade. The large boat's hull was made of dark wood. Walnut, maybe.

The Frenchwoman shaded her eyes against the late afternoon sun as she called to someone behind the helm on a higher deck. A motor started and then the boat was off. Sam's heart slumped as they pulled away from the island. She had so hoped Billie and Garth or the no-show bodyguard would come to her rescue. Not to mention Derek.

"Can you tell me where we're going now?"

"St. Thomas."

"To the Blanca Institute, no doubt."

"That's right," he said, lighting a cigarette.

"Could you go somewhere else to smoke?"

"And leave you alone to swim back to shore?"

She looked wistfully at the shrinking island and cruise ship. Between the pirate boat and shore were already three distinctly different colored strips of water. Deep blue close to shore, a light green in the middle, and a gorgeous turquoise around the boat. She pointed at her stomach. "Do you really think I could make it back to shore? Seems I'd be doing you a favor by diving into the water."

He motioned to all of the little sailboats in the bay, his cigarette leaving a trail of smoke. "And take a chance of one of these sailors fishing you out?"

Suddenly the notion of jumping into the water held added appeal. "At least blow your smoke over the side."

Warren moved back until he was leaning against the railing. "Better?"

When he had taken a last drag and flicked the butt into the Caribbean, Sam asked, "Who are you? I take it your name's not really Warren Pruett."

He tightened the blanket around Tiffany's legs.

Sam watched a dirty-blond boy hoist the white sheets. The spinnaker—she knew the name of the headsail because it was also the name of the restaurant in Sausalito where John had proposed—was orange. She wondered if she'd be seeing John before Derek. "You were in Denver at the airport, now you're here. Who are you?"

"Who do you think I am?" You'd think she was on Jeopardy or something.

"I have no idea."

The Frenchwoman stood beside the brown-haired man at the wheel, her lightweight print coverup puffed with wind. The tail of the coverup snapped like the canvas sails, showing her white bikini bottoms, a great deal of crack, and roll after roll of fat on her thighs. It wasn't an altogether pleasant sight.

"How would it hurt if you told me your name? You aren't going to let me live. I know you killed Doyle Smith and Alan Martin."

"I didn't kill Alan Martin. I am Alan Martin."

"Harvard Medical School class of sixty-two Alan Martin?"

He nodded.

"You died in a two-car accident involving four teenagers."

"Who told you that?"

"Doyle Smith's mother."

"She's mistaken."

"That's a pretty big mistake to make."

"Tiffany may have inspired it. Saying you divorced your husband to marry his golf partner doesn't play as well, does it?"

"And Doyle let her lie to his mother like that?"

"Doyle went along with almost everything she said."

Almost. "What was in his letter?"

"A smart woman like you should have figured that out by now."

"That Sean MacCade was impersonating you?"

"It figured in. Sean was a good technician. He could have been a doctor had he been given the chance."

"And you gave him the chance."

"The family planning clinic in Denver simply couldn't provide the number of ah . . . donations needed. Central LA was the perfect location for a second clinic. You could say that I practiced medicine in two places at the same time."

"Donations? Is that what you call it? Women come to the clinics for abortions and contraception and you relieve them of their eggs?" That's what Doyle's letter had to be about.

"Only those wanting permanent sterilization. We don't charge them. It's all free."

A real stand-up guy! "Do you tell them that they will need a synthetic estrogen for the rest of their lives, or do you let them figure it out for themselves?" It was a rhetorical question. Both of them knew it. "You killed Doyle to keep him from going to the authorities. But why did you bomb the LA clinic and kill Sean?"

"He panicked, wanted out. Said your husband came to see him after Doyle's death. That he knew he was there when Doyle died. What good was the clinic without him? It seemed as good a way as any to destroy the records."

"Why was Sean at the convention?"

"The three of us tried to convince Doyle to see the light. He was so pigheaded. Doyle had already contacted the authorities, had he? That's why the CIA was there."

Was it to her advantage or disadvantage to correct him? Tiffany's head had fallen forward. Sam tilted it back. "Why were you on the ship with Tiffany?"

"It seemed the easiest way to get her home. Who would question it? Patients going to and from the Blanca Institute are a weekly occurrence. I had hoped to return her to Denver and resume our life the way it was before Doyle spoiled everything. But it looks like we might have to change our plans. Rio has a nice climate."

"Catholics aren't noted for practicing birth control. They

won't be lining up in front of your new clinic."

"Doyle ruined everything. Tiffany knew it, too."

Murders aside, he wasn't altogether rational. He had a real thing for Tiffany and probably enjoyed killing his good ol' golfing buddy. "Why was Tiffany here in the first place?"

He found another cigarette. "She had already realized Doyle wasn't the answer to her dreams, but she went ballistic over her brother's death. Came down here and threatened to go to the authorities herself if Pounce Blanca didn't take care of me. Of course, he called me to come get her. By the time I arrived the butcher had done this to her. He needed precursors for two patients."

Billie and Vivian. "What's a person to do when his supplies have been cut in half with the closure of the LA clinic?" She'd wished she hadn't made the flippant remark. He looked angry.

"You don't seem to understand the significance of our work." He was fingering his gun, but she knew he wouldn't dare kill her here.

"Steal from the poor, sell to the rich. You think I have a problem understanding the significance of that?"

"Being poor isn't a prerequisite. We gladly take all donations. Look at you. Not only will you help with our depleted supply of precursors, but you'll furnish islet cells."

Now the reason Paul was dead and she wasn't was all too clear. He needed her baby. The scream came through her like a runaway train.

$\triangledown$

36

DEREK RUBBED THE sharp stubble on his cheek as he hurried to the pier. There hadn't been time to clean up after his plane landed in Miami, not if he wanted to meet Samantha when the ship docked. It had been a grueling sixty-eight hours in eastern Europe and all he wanted now was to collect his wife and go home.

He was in time to watch the dockworker wrap the thick rope around the anvil as if it were child's play. The ship was settled in its berth. The immigration inspector boarded. It was when two plainclothesmen and two uniformed policemen went aboard that the alarm went off. That was not routine.

Derek raced inside to the bank of phones and called the ranch. There were two messages on the recording. One for Samantha to call the hospital lab for her messages, the other for him to check in. He called the hospital first. Would anyone be there on a Sunday? A woman answered after ten rings.

"This is Derek Turner, Dr. Turner's husband."

"Oh, yes, I'm Kristy, we had coffee—"

"Yes, I remember. She's asked me to call for her messages."

"You sound so far away."

"We're in Miami. The messages?"

"Just a minute."

No one was coming off the ship, yet. The static-charged music ended and Kristy was back.

"She has a whole slew of them."

"Let's hear them."

"Here's one from Lieutenant Javiar Gomez, Miami Police Department. Ask for Homicide."

Homicide sent up a red flag, but the message was for Samantha, not about her. "What else?"

"Here's one to call a Billie Wade . . . do you think that's *the* Billie Wade?"

A confirmation. Both good and bad. Billie Wade wouldn't be calling if she were on the ship with him, nor would he have called if she were the victim. "Probably lots of people with that name. Anything else?"

"Here's one attached to a denim jumper."

The perfume-soaked jumper lost on the doomed airplane? "What about it?"

"Says that someone found it a couple of miles from the crash site. Said there was a name tag in the pocket, for a Chris Newman from San Francisco. Said one of the investigators called Newman and was told that the jumper was Dr. Turner's. Then it says that he said that she got the scrap of paper out of a wastepaper basket."

"What scrap of paper?"

"Just a minute . . . ouch . . . found the name tag. Here it is. It's a phone number."

"Can you read it to me?" She rattled off the numbers. "No area code?"

"That's it."

"Anything else on the paper?"

"Nothing."

He made the second call to hear Carole apologize for not reaching Scotty with the message about sending someone to watch Samantha. Scotty was in South America.

"Carole, I need a favor."

"Name it."

"Run a check on a phone number." He gave her the number.

"Area code?"

"Don't have one."

"You never were easy."

"Start with southern California, Colorado, and Florida. We're looking for something to do with medicine."

He gave her the number of the neighboring pay phone. His next call was to Woods. Samantha wasn't in St. Thomas as far as Woods knew. Nothing unusual was happening there. One patient came by taxi, even though the new batch wasn't expected until the ship landed. Derek was looking at the ship now. Woods had talked with a cook at the institute, but didn't get much information, just praise for the administrator, Pounce Blanca. Was making twice the salary as the last job.

"Could the patient have been my wife?"

"Looking at the report I'd say no. Thin young woman in a wheelchair, very pale."

No one would call his wife thin. The phone next door rang. "Hold on, that's for me." He picked up the second phone, "Turner, here."

"Derek, I think I've got something."

"Shoot."

"The area code is 303. The number is a residence line in Denver, but it also terminates off-premise at the Westside Family Planning Center. The listing is for Alan Martin."

"Is it a working or disconnected number?"

"Working."

Alan Martin had both a car and a current telephone number. How dead was this guy?

"Send someone to go through both his home and the clinic in search of my wife. Samantha shouldn't be hard to spot, she's seven months pregnant."

"You never told me you were married. Samantha Turner." There was a moment of silence. "Here it is. She's pretty. My!"

"What?"

"Her driving record."

"Carole, you and your computer are amazing. Are you sending her driver's license picture to Denver?"

"No, the one on her California medical license renewal looks the clearest."

"She still has a California license?"

"Yeah."

"Look up Alan Martin's driver's license and California and Colorado medical licenses and fax his picture to Lieutenant Javiar Gomez, Homicide, Miami Police Department."

"Got it." He was having trouble hearing her. The disembarking passengers were fanning out over the pier like the Mississippi Delta.

"I'll drop by next time I'm in town. You can show me Samantha's file."

"Have to buy me coffee first."

"It's a deal."

"Anything else?"

"That's it. Big thanks." He picked up the other phone. "I'll call you back when I have more details."

Lieutenant Javiar Gomez wasn't hard to spot standing next to the ship's captain. They'd sequestered witnesses and turned the Pirate's Cove Lounge into an interrogation room. Cherry was the one Derek wouldn't have recognized. Her hair was entirely brown and cut in a sleek pageboy. And she clung to Billie like an ardent lover. Judd, Gracie, Garth, and Vivian sat in the booth with them. Officers sat in the next booth. Two stewards, maître d' Mario, and waiter Favio sat at a small table near the bar. Warren Pruett and Samantha were missing.

Derek pulled out his credentials once again, but this time it wasn't his press card. The Miami policeman at the lounge's threshold called over the lieutenant.

The lieutenant glanced at the ID and closed it as he handed it back to Derek. "Explains the helicopter. Can you explain the corpse found in your stateroom?"

"Warren Pruett?"

Javiar shook his head slowly. "Paul Baskin."

"The steward? No. What about my wife?"

The lieutenant shrugged. "Would like to talk to her for starters."

Derek gestured to the booth of passengers. "Have you taken their statements?"

Javiar gave him an after-you gesture. "You'll be able to catch up."

"So here you are," Billie said as he scooted in to make room for Derek.

Cherry leaned across Billie to have her say. "I don't think Samantha killed Paul." She had a wholesome dotting of freckles across the bridge of her nose. Derek marveled at the transformation. Ordinarily it would have made him suspicious.

"Nor do I," Derek responded. He caught Judd's eye.

The old Texan's crinkled face was set hard, his eyes had lost their smile. "She's gone, boy. We didn't do our job. We've looked in every nook and cranny."

Lieutenant Gomez seemed comfortable letting Derek be the center of attention. "The Pruetts?"

"They're gone, too."

"Who saw Samantha last?"

Garth raised his hand. "I walked her back to the ship."

"They were with Cherry and Warren and me on the Dutch side of St. Maarten," Billie explained. He put his hand over his mouth and said in a low voice, "She was acting very strange."

"Beg your pardon?" Gomez didn't let that one get by.

"She wasn't feeling well," Billie told him.

"I walked back with her," Garth continued. "She was tired and wanted to come back to the ship. She left me in the Lido Lounge to go to her cabin to rest."

"What about Warren?"

Cherry answered. "He left a couple of stores later. Said he was going back to the ship for lunch."

Gracie nodded. "Judd and I ate lunch with him."

"How about dinner?"

Judd shook his head. "That's when we missed them."

"Billie ordered and left the table to fetch Samantha," Cherry explained. "That's when they found poor Paul."

"Who let you in, Billie?"

He pointed to one of the stewards. "While he was calling the purser I went down to the Pruett's stateroom. There was a Do Not Disturb sign, but I knocked anyway. No one answered."

"Did any of you actually see Warren or his wife at the Blanca Institute in St. Thomas?" Derek asked.

"I didn't." Billed beamed at his wife. "Did you, sweetheart?"

"Not that I remember, sugar."

Derek felt more comfortable with them when they were fighting. "He came on in St. Thomas with you. When did you first meet him?"

"Outside the dining room that first night. Came up and introduced himself, said we had mutual friends—the Kramers."

"When did you first meet him, Judd?"

Judd gave it some thought. "At the Institute. He came into Gracie's room one night and asked Gracie how she was feeling."

"Was that Warren?" Gracie asked. "I took him for a doctor—though he didn't actually introduce himself."

"Did anyone see his wife there?" Derek asked.

No one could remember seeing her.

Garth started to say something, then didn't.

"What is it, Garth?"

"Let me preface this by saying that I have nothing but praise for the Blanca Institute. But . . . I can understand why they would want to isolate her from the rest of us. It wouldn't be good PR. I don't believe the treatment worked for her."

"That would explain why she never left her cabin," Billie said. "Heaven knows I didn't feel like seeing anyone before my treatment."

"How do you know it didn't work?" Derek asked.

"I don't really. She was in a wheelchair and looked pale. Though redheads are often light-complected."

"Redhead?"

$\triangledown$

37

A_S DEREK PASSED the nurses' station, he tugged at the shoulder of the white industrial jumpsuit. It was stiff and smelled faintly of bleach.

The coffee-skinned nurse stopped twisting a strand of long mahogany hair and secured it behind her ear with a shiny barrette. "What are you doing here?"

Looking for Tiffany to ask her what happened to Samantha and Warren, aka Alan Martin: it was Warren's picture that came off the fax machine at the Miami Police Department. Derek looked down at his clipboard. "Says there's a leak in the propane line."

"I wasn't told about a leak."

"Says I'm to find and fix it." He turned and started down the hall.

She rounded the counter and ran after him. "You can't come through here and disturb our patients. It's the middle of the night. Have the security guard take you around to the service entrance. How'd you get past him, anyway?"

Derek had simply left him in the bushes. "He told me to come in alone," Derek said over his shoulder as he kept moving toward the patients' rooms. "Some punk's messing with him."

"Stop right there."

He stopped in front of a swank sitting room. The Caribbean-blue Oriental rug had to be worth a fortune. A gold couch and matching love seat sat in front of a wall of white shutters. A center shutter was folded back, revealing a balcony and the top of a coconut tree. The clinic was on a slope.

Derek got a good whiff of La Fleuri Parfum as she barred his way, and felt he was that much closer to finding Tiffany and, more importantly, Samantha.

"Nice smell. That would go over in a big way with the wife. Where can I get some?"

She shook her head. "Don't know. This was a gift."

"From someone around here?"

"A patient from the United States." Her eyes grew to saucers as Derek clapped his hand over her mouth and pulled her tight against him.

"Take me to her and you won't get hurt. Understand?"

She nodded.

"Start moving." He felt, more than heard, her mouth moving against the palm of his hand. "This way?" She nodded. "One of these rooms?" She nodded again. "Move your feet."

She shuffled down the corridor, Derek her Siamese twin. She stopped in front of a door. He dragged her into the room.

His wife, not Tiffany, was gagged and strapped to the bed railing. An IV line ran into her right arm. Her eyes were wild with excitement. Derek pitched the clipboard onto the Edwardian chair. He and the nurse moved to the bed. He dug his elbow into the nurse's sternum as he ripped off the tape from Samantha's mouth.

"You've got to get me out of here."

Derek smoothed the tape over the nurse's mouth. "Don't move." He was speaking to the nurse; Samantha couldn't move. "What are they doing to you?" he asked as he untied her hands.

She ripped out the IV and pulled the end of a catheter out from under the sheets. She tossed it over the side of the bed, spraying urine on the carpet. "They're inducing labor. I'll explain later, just get me out of here."

Derek slide his arms around her back and lifted her off

the bed. A sharp pain seized her before her feet touched ground. A heavy sheen of perspiration masked her face. "You all right?"

"We will be if you can get me out of here."

He pushed the nurse onto the bed and bound her wrists with Samantha's terrycloth strips.

Samantha wrestled the lightweight blanket out from under the nurse and yanked it free. She wrapped it around her hospital gown. She moaned and leaned against the bed. "Are you all right, Samantha?"

"The baby's coming... get me out of here." She took two faltering steps toward the door. "Take the barrettes out of her hair and get the sheet."

He went back for them. She doubled over again. "How far apart are the contractions?"

"They aren't."

"What does that mean?"

"We have to hurry. I can't have the baby here."

He swooped her into his arms. "Woods is waiting with the van at the top of the hill."

"How are we going to get up the hill?"

It was a good question, one he'd asked himself. "We'll manage," he said with more confidence than he felt. Derek backtracked around the corner when the big black security guard staggered through the front door, ruefully rubbing his neck. "Do you know another way out?"

She shut her eyes tight and bit her lip. Another contraction. He held her securely and headed back the way they'd come to a door at the end of the corridor. It opened onto a concrete stairwell. He headed up, away from the steady whine of a generator.

"They'll kill the baby for the islet cells if they find us."

"I won't let that happen."

Her tears fell on his neck. "It would have already happened if it hadn't been for Tiffany. They would have cut me open and performed an oophorectomy but Alan wanted to demonstrate a superlative technique. He put me on a drip. I thought you were dead in the streets of South America."

"I was in Europe. Where's Tiffany?"

"In one of the other rooms. I don't know."

They could look for her later; getting Samantha to a safe hospital was his immediate concern. He took the next few steps to the landing at a run. The door below was opening. Derek stepped back into the shadows, feeling rough concrete against his back. He pulled Samantha's head tightly to his chest as her next contraction came. Her sweat-slick fingers drilled into his shoulders.

"Check the boiler room and the roof." The voice had a slight Latino accent. "We'll look in the operating suites." Derek waited until the guard raced down the stairs and into the boiler room before ascending to the roof.

The door opened onto a flat graveled surface. The drop oceanside was two stories. Hillside offered a steep tiled roof. They were in dense palm-tree cover. If he wanted help—and he did—he'd have to traverse the roof for Woods to see him. The moon illuminating the sea would be going behind a cloud shortly. Before signaling Woods, he had to deal with the security guard. Again.

"I'm afraid my dear, this is where we'll make our stand."

"What about the baby? They'll kill the baby." She was drenched in sweat.

He placed her against the wall, at the far corner, away from the door. If the security guard came crashing through, she would have a degree of protection. "They'll have to kill me first."

"Boy, does that comfort me!" She unwrapped the blanket and leaned over her abdomen. "I'm at the wrong end to deliver this baby. Can you see the baby's head yet?"

"Yes, I see the head." He squeezed assurance into her knee. "Samantha, the security guard will be here any minute . . . as soon as he sees that we're not in the boiler room. It's your choice. Do I cross the roof to signal Woods or stay and help you?"

"Signal Woods, for petesakes."

He kissed her soaking forehead. "I'll be right back."

She grunted and pushed for all she was worth. "Der . . . clips."

Derek fished the barrettes out of his starched overalls and folded them into the palm of her hand. "I love you."

She shook her head, nodded, and then gritted her teeth and bore down. "Go." He forced himself away.

Derek cracked the door open, but heard and saw nothing. He closed the door, ripped off his shoes and socks, and took a running leap to the tile roof. He missed the apex and slid down, damp tiles slipping away beneath his helplessly clawing fingers. His legs dropped over the edge and dangled uselessly, but his hands gripped the gutter. It would be a simple matter to drop off and run up the hill to where Woods was waiting. But then Samantha would be alone.

He swung his right leg up and hoisted himself back onto the roof. He moved hand over hand along the rooftop, ducking around a skylight. He crawled up the next slope of tiles to achieve the apex. A loose tile clanged and clattered over the edge loud enough to wake the devil himself. He eased his way along the apex until he was beyond the tree and within Woods's sights.

Derek struck a match. He held it high until his fingertips were seared, and then tossed it. He struck another. And in the end, sent it sailing. The third match lit the cover. When it was aglow, he tossed it high overhead and watched the tiny flare turn to ashes as it fell to earth.

A bullet whistled by. He scrambled over the apex. Samantha's scream echoing in his ear. The trip back across the front side of the rooftop took only a fraction of the time, but worry made it twice as long.

His best plan of attack was to circle back and outflank the gunman. He crawled to the end of the building, whipped off his belt, and slid along the ledge. He crouched in the shadow of the eave, winding the belt twice around his left hand. With a hollow thud, Derek landed on the graveled surface just behind the security guard. He lashed the belt around a thick neck and snapped it up and back. A .38 fell to the gravel first.

"No, Derek, he's on our side!"

Derek held the pressure constant.

"He didn't know they were baby killers. He's guarding the door for us."

Derek picked up the weapon and then freed the belt. The guard gasped for air. "I expected to be a father by now," he said as he dropped between Samantha's knees.

"I'm doing the best I can." She drew breath. "Much harder being the mother . . . than the doctor."

"What should I do?"

She panted. "Apologize to him and tell me what you see."

Derek held out the .38. "Sorry."

"No problem," the guard said hoarsely, rubbing his neck.

Derek opened a leg to what little moonlight hadn't gone behind the clouds. "The head is right—"

She clawed at his shoulders and cried out. He looked away a moment as he heard the commotion at the door.

"No problem," the guard assured them as he threw his massive body against the banging door.

"Big problem," Derek mumbled. "It's coming. Push harder."

She strained and dug her fingernails into his shoulders. Then she relaxed and threw her head back. "I can't."

"You can."

Her breath came in rapid shallow gasps.

"Breathe deeply," he said in what he hoped sounded like a controlled voice. "Now, let it out slowly."

She obeyed until another contraction took her. She screamed and pushed. Skin ripped as the head protruded. Derek's mind was numb with fear—not of the men at the door, but of this tiny creature. He slid shaking hands under the head but didn't dare touch it.

The guard had disappeared. Samantha was crying. "One more push." She held her breath and pushed. The push petered out into sobs. "A little more, Samantha, the head isn't all the way out." She screamed and pushed. The skin tore deeper as the head came toward his hands. Blood matted the hair. "Push!"

"I am pushing!" she screamed back.

"Well, do it better."

Anger gave her the edge. She held her breath and pushed for all she was worth. The head popped out in a gush of fluid. The wrinkled face was covered in what looked like white lotion streaked with blood. The eyes were closed tight. The mouth twisted with fierce determination and let rip a mighty protest. Derek could do no more than cup his hands and hold them under this new being, catching drips. He raised hands that no longer seemed part of his body and allowed the back of the head to tickle his palms.

"Is it a girl?" Samantha asked as she strained to look.

"I don't know yet." It all happened so quickly that he didn't know when his hands took control, but he was nudging first one and then the other thin shoulder through. "Push again, Mom."

"Run your finger around the inside of her mouth to get out any mucous," she said as she pushed half-heartedly.

"You can do better than that."

"I've lost the urge . . . pull."

Derek eased fingers under the lilliputian armpits and tugged timidly. He yanked harder as the bloody little thing hollered like the town crier. He wasn't any happier to be here than they were. His scrawny body plopped out in front of another gush of fluid, his twig legs kicking into the world. "It's a boy, Samantha. It's a boy."

"A boy," she repeated in tearful joy.

Sirens and flashing red lights celebrated his son's birth.

"He needs to be lower than the cord." Mom was now doctor.

"I don't think I can manage that. You're already on the ground. Shall I wrap him up?"

"The blood needs to drain into his body." She reached behind her and pulled out the sheet. "Here," she said, spreading it out over her swollen middle. He placed the screamer in the middle of the sheet and wrapped him with care. He lowered the baby to just above the wet graveled floor.

Samantha gave the cord between her legs a hefty tug, and then held it high to give gravity a helping hand. She flailed around for the barrettes. "Here—place them about two inches apart somewhere close to the baby—not too close, though, it'll have to be redone later. Do you have your knife?"

Derek nodded. "Of course."

"Good. Use it."

He needed more hands. He scooted around until he was sitting Indian-style in the wet puddle and cradled the baby in his legs. "He's so tiny," he said over the baby's wails.

"We have to get him to the hospital." She looked around. "Where's what's-his-name?"

Derek shook his head. "Don't know." He fought with the first barrette. The second clipped on easier. The knife was deep in his pocket and the baby cried in protest as he shifted for it. "Cut between them, I take it?"

"Of course."

"Didn't know. Monahseetah and I skipped this part."

"Give me the baby while you deliver the placenta."

Derek turned to see Woods. "Everything all right?"

Woods gagged and looked away. "The fat lady's done singing. I'll call an ambulance."

"Tell them we'll need an incubator," Samantha added softly as she cradled the baby in her arms.

Woods hurried away.

The clouds passed and the moonlight over the calm sea brightened. The baby quieted and the rooftop transformed into a peaceful paradise for three.

"He has dark hair, Derek."

Derek caught her eye. He knew what she was driving at. Blond hair is a recessive trait; two blonds could produce only a blond offspring. Jeffrey and Samantha were both blond. Derek was the father.

"Didn't matter."

FIC
LANDR

Landreth, Marsha.

A clinic for murder.

533515

DATE			

WEST GEORGIA REGIONAL LIBRARY SYSTEM
Neva Lomason Memorial Library

BAKER & TAYLOR BOOKS